# A Hero of Our Time

## M. Y. Lermontov

# FOREWORD

THIS novel, known as one of the masterpieces of Russian Literature, under the title "A Hero of our Time," and already translated into at least nine European languages, is now for the first time placed before the general English Reader.

The work is of exceptional interest to the student of English Literature, written as it was under the profound influence of Byron and being itself a study of the Byronic type of character.

The Translators have taken especial care to preserve both the atmosphere of the story and the poetic beauty with which the Poet-novelist imbued his pages.

# CONTENTS

# BOOK I

# BELA

# THE HEART OF A RUSSIAN

## CHAPTER I

I was travelling post from Tiflis.

All the luggage I had in my cart consisted of one small portmanteau half filled with travelling-notes on Georgia; of these the greater part has been lost, fortunately for you; but the portmanteau itself and the rest of its contents have remained intact, fortunately for me.

As I entered the Koishaur Valley the sun was disappearing behind the snow-clad ridge of the mountains. In order to accomplish the ascent of Mount Koishaur by nightfall, my driver, an Ossete, urged on the horses indefatigably, singing zealously the while at the top of his voice.

What a glorious place that valley is! On every hand are inaccessible mountains, steep, yellow slopes scored by water-channels, and reddish rocks draped with green ivy and crowned with clusters of plane-trees. Yonder, at an immense height, is the golden fringe of the snow. Down below rolls the River Aragva, which, after bursting noisily forth from the dark and misty depths of the gorge, with an unnamed stream clasped in its embrace, stretches out like a thread of silver, its waters glistening like a snake with flashing scales.

Arrived at the foot of Mount Koishaur, we stopped at a dukhan. [1] About a score of Georgians and mountaineers were gathered there in a noisy crowd, and, close by, a caravan of camels had halted for the night. I was obliged to hire oxen to drag my cart up that accursed mountain, as it was now autumn and the roads were slippery with ice. Besides, the mountain is about two versts [2] in length.

---

[1] A retail shop and tavern combined
[2] A verst is a measure of length, about 3500 English feet.

There was no help for it, so I hired six oxen and a few Ossetes. One of the latter shouldered my portmanteau, and the rest, shouting almost with one voice, proceeded to help the oxen.

Following mine there came another cart, which I was surprised to see four oxen pulling with the greatest ease, notwithstanding that it was loaded to the top. Behind it walked the owner, smoking a little, silver-mounted Kabardian pipe. He was wearing a shaggy Circassian cap and an officer's overcoat without epaulettes, and he seemed to be about fifty years of age. The swarthiness of his complexion showed that his face had long been acquainted with Transcaucasian suns, and the premature greyness of his moustache was out of keeping with his firm gait and robust appearance. I went up to him and saluted. He silently returned my greeting and emitted an immense cloud of smoke.

"We are fellow-travellers, it appears."

Again he bowed silently.

"I suppose you are going to Stavropol?"

"Yes, sir, exactly—with Government things."

"Can you tell me how it is that that heavily-laden cart of yours is being drawn without any difficulty by four oxen, whilst six cattle are scarcely able to move mine, empty though it is, and with all those Ossetes helping?"

He smiled slyly and threw me a meaning glance.

"You have not been in the Caucasus long, I should say?"

"About a year," I answered.

He smiled a second time.

"Well?"

"Just so, sir," he answered. "They're terrible beasts, these Asiatics! You think that all that shouting means that they are helping the oxen? Why, the devil alone can make out what it is they do shout. The oxen understand, though; and if you were to yoke as many as twenty they still wouldn't budge so long as the Ossetes shouted in that way of theirs.... Awful scoundrels! But what can you make of them? They love extorting money from people who happen to be travelling through here. The rogues have been spoiled! You wait and see: they will get a tip out of you as well as their hire. I know them of old, they can't get round me!"

2

"You have been serving here a long time?"

"Yes, I was here under Aleksei Petrovich," [3] he answered, assuming an air of dignity. "I was a sub-lieutenant when he came to the Line; and I was promoted twice, during his command, on account of actions against the mountaineers."

"And now—?"

"Now I'm in the third battalion of the Line. And you yourself?"

I told him.

With this the conversation ended, and we continued to walk in silence, side by side. On the summit of the mountain we found snow. The sun set, and— as usually is the case in the south—night followed upon the day without any interval of twilight. Thanks, however, to the sheen of the snow, we were able easily to distinguish the road, which still went up the mountain-side, though not so steeply as before. I ordered the Ossetes to put my portmanteau into the cart, and to replace the oxen by horses. Then for the last time I gazed down upon the valley; but the thick mist which had gushed in billows from the gorges veiled it completely, and not a single sound now floated up to our ears from below. The Ossetes surrounded me clamorously and demanded tips; but the staff-captain shouted so menacingly at them that they dispersed in a moment.

"What a people they are!" he said. "They don't even know the Russian for 'bread,' but they have mastered the phrase 'Officer, give us a tip!' In my opinion, the very Tartars are better, they are no drunkards, anyhow."...

We were now within a verst or so of the Station. Around us all was still, so still, indeed, that it was possible to follow the flight of a gnat by the buzzing of its wings. On our left loomed the gorge, deep and black. Behind it and in front of us rose the dark-blue summits of the mountains, all trenched with furrows and covered with layers of snow, and standing out against the pale horizon, which still retained the last reflections of the evening glow. The stars twinkled out in the dark sky, and in some strange way it seemed to me that they were much higher than in our own north country. On both sides of the road bare, black rocks jutted out; here and there shrubs peeped forth from under the snow; but not a single withered leaf stirred, and amid

---

[3] Ermolov, i.e. General Ermolov. Russians have three names—Christian name, patronymic and surname. They are addressed by the first two only. The surname of Maksim Maksimych (colloquial for Maksimovich) is not mentioned.

that dead sleep of nature it was cheering to hear the snorting of the three tired post-horses and the irregular tinkling of the Russian bell. [4]

"We will have glorious weather to-morrow," I said.

The staff-captain answered not a word, but pointed with his finger to a lofty mountain which rose directly opposite us.

"What is it?" I asked.

"Mount Gut."
"Well, what then?"

"Don't you see how it is smoking?"

True enough, smoke was rising from Mount Gut. Over its sides gentle cloud-currents were creeping, and on the summit rested one cloud of such dense blackness that it appeared like a blot upon the dark sky.

By this time we were able to make out the Post Station and the roofs of the huts surrounding it; the welcoming lights were twinkling before us, when suddenly a damp and chilly wind arose, the gorge rumbled, and a drizzling rain fell. I had scarcely time to throw my felt cloak round me when down came the snow. I looked at the staff-captain with profound respect.

"We shall have to pass the night here," he said, vexation in his tone. "There's no crossing the mountains in such a blizzard.—I say, have there been any avalanches on Mount Krestov?" he inquired of the driver.

"No, sir," the Ossete answered; "but there are a great many threatening to fall—a great many."

Owing to the lack of a travellers' room in the Station, we were assigned a night's lodging in a smoky hut. I invited my fellow-traveller to drink a tumbler of tea with me, as I had brought my cast-iron teapot—my only solace during my travels in the Caucasus.

One side of the hut was stuck against the cliff, and three wet and slippery steps led up to the door. I groped my way in and stumbled up against a cow (with these people the cow-house supplies the place of a servant's room). I did not know which way to turn—sheep were bleating on the one hand and a dog growling on the other. Fortunately, however, I perceived on one side a faint glimmer of light, and by its aid I was able to find another opening by way of a door. And here a by no means uninteresting picture was revealed.

---

[4] The bell on the duga, a wooden arch joining the shafts of a Russian conveyance over the horse's neck.

4

The wide hut, the roof of which rested on two smoke-grimed pillars, was full of people. In the center of the floor a small fire was crackling, and the smoke, driven back by the wind from an opening in the roof, was spreading around in so thick a shroud that for a long time I was unable to see about me. Seated by the fire were two old women, a number of children and a lank Georgian—all of them in tatters. There was no help for it! We took refuge by the fire and lighted our pipes; and soon the teapot was singing invitingly.

"Wretched people, these!" I said to the staff-captain, indicating our dirty hosts, who were silently gazing at us in a kind of torpor.

"And an utterly stupid people too!" he replied. "Would you believe it, they are absolutely ignorant and incapable of the slightest civilisation! Why even our Kabardians or Chechenes, robbers and ragamuffins though they be, are regular dare-devils for all that. Whereas these others have no liking for arms, and you'll never see a decent dagger on one of them! Ossetes all over!"

"You have been a long time in the Chechenes' country?"

"Yes, I was quartered there for about ten years along with my company in a fortress, near Kamennyi Brod. 5 Do you know the place?"

"I have heard the name."

"I can tell you, my boy, we had quite enough of those dare-devil Chechenes. At the present time, thank goodness, things are quieter; but in the old days you had only to put a hundred paces between you and the rampart and wherever you went you would be sure to find a shaggy devil lurking in wait for you. You had just to let your thoughts wander and at any moment a lasso would be round your neck or a bullet in the back of your head! Brave fellows, though!"...

"You used to have many an adventure, I dare say?" I said, spurred by curiosity.

"Of course! Many a one."...

Hereupon he began to tug at his left moustache, let his head sink on to his breast, and became lost in thought. I had a very great mind to extract some little anecdote out of him—a desire natural to all who travel and make notes.

Meanwhile, tea was ready. I took two travelling-tumblers out of my

---

5 Rocky Ford.

portmanteau, and, filling one of them, set it before the staff-captain. He sipped his tea and said, as if speaking to himself, "Yes, many a one!" This exclamation gave me great hopes. Your old Caucasian officer loves, I know, to talk and yarn a bit; he so rarely succeeds in getting a chance to do so. It may be his fate to be quartered five years or so with his company in some out-of-the-way place, and during the whole of that time he will not hear "good morning" from a soul (because the sergeant says "good health"). And, indeed, he would have good cause to wax loquacious—with a wild and interesting people all around him, danger to be faced every day, and many a marvelous incident happening. It is in circumstances like this that we involuntarily complain that so few of our countrymen take notes.

"Would you care to put some rum in your tea?" I said to my companion. "I have some white rum with me—from Tiflis; and the weather is cold now."

"No, thank you, sir; I don't drink."

"Really?"

"Just so. I have sworn off drinking. Once, you know, when I was a sub-lieutenant, some of us had a drop too much. That very night there was an alarm, and out we went to the front, half seas over! We did catch it, I can tell you, when Aleksei Petrovich came to hear about us! Heaven save us, what a rage he was in! He was within an ace of having us court-martialled. That's just how things happen! You might easily spend a whole year without seeing a soul; but just go and have a drop and you're a lost man!"

On hearing this I almost lost hope.

"Take the Circassians, now," he continued; "once let them drink their fill of buza [6] at a wedding or a funeral, and out will come their knives. On one occasion I had some difficulty in getting away with a whole skin, and yet it was at the house of a 'friendly' [7] prince, where I was a guest, that the affair happened."

"How was that?" I asked.

"Here, I'll tell you."...

He filled his pipe, drew in the smoke, and began his story.

---

[6] A kind of beer made from millet.

[7] i.e. acknowledging Russian supremacy.

# CHAPTER II

"YOU see, sir," said the staff-captain, "I was quartered, at the time, with a company in a fortress beyond the Terek—getting on for five years ago now. One autumn day, a transport arrived with provisions, in charge of an officer, a young man of about twenty-five. He reported himself to me in full uniform, and announced that he had been ordered to remain in the fortress with me. He was so very elegant, his complexion so nice and white, his uniform so brand new, that I immediately guessed that he had not been long with our army in the Caucasus.

"'I suppose you have been transferred from Russia?' I asked.

"'Exactly, captain,' he answered.

"I took him by the hand and said:

"'I'm delighted to see you—delighted! It will be a bit dull for you... but there, we will live together like a couple of friends. But, please, call me simply "Maksim Maksimych"; and, tell me, what is this full uniform for? Just wear your forage-cap whenever you come to me!'

"Quarters were assigned to him and he settled down in the fortress."

"What was his name?" I asked Maksim Maksimych.

"His name was Grigori Aleksandrovich Pechorin. He was a splendid fellow, I can assure you, but a little peculiar. Why, to give you an instance, one time he would stay out hunting the whole day, in the rain and cold; the others would all be frozen through and tired out, but he wouldn't mind either cold or fatigue. Then, another time, he would be sitting in his own room, and, if there was a breath of wind, he would declare that he had caught cold; if the shutters rattled against the window he would start and turn pale: yet I myself have seen him attack a boar single-handed. Often enough you couldn't drag a word out of him for hours together; but then, on the other hand, sometimes, when he started telling stories, you would split your sides with laughing. Yes, sir, a very eccentric man; and he must have been wealthy too. What a lot of expensive trinkets he had!"...

"Did he stay there long with you?" I went on to ask.

"Yes, about a year. And, for that very reason, it was a memorable year to me. He gave me a great deal of trouble—but there, let bygones be

7

bygones!... You see, it is true enough, there are people like that, fated from birth to have all sorts of strange things happening to them!"

"Strange?" I exclaimed, with an air of curiosity, as I poured out some tea.

# CHAPTER III

"WELL, then, I'll tell you," said Maksim Maksimych. "About six versts from the fortress there lived a certain 'friendly' prince. His son, a brat of about fifteen, was accustomed to ride over to visit us. Not a day passed but he would come, now for one thing, now for another. And, indeed, Grigori Aleksandrovich and I spoiled him. What a dare-devil the boy was! Up to anything, picking up a cap at full gallop, or bringing things down with his gun! He had one bad quality; he was terribly greedy for money. Once, for the fun of the thing, Grigori Aleksandrovich promised to give him a ducat if he would steal the best he-goat from his father's herd for him; and, what do you think? The very next night he came lugging it in by the horns! At times we used to take it into our heads to tease him, and then his eyes would become bloodshot and his hand would fly to his dagger immediately.

"'You'll be losing your life if you are not careful, Azamat,' I would say to him. 'That hot head of yours will get you into trouble.'

"On one occasion, the old prince himself came to invite us to the wedding of his eldest daughter; and, as we were guest-friends with him, it was impossible to decline, Tartar though he was. We set off. In the village we were met by a number of dogs, all barking loudly. The women, when they saw us coming, hid themselves, but those whose faces we were able to get a view of were far from being beauties.

"'I had a much better opinion of the Circassian women,' remarked Grigori Aleksandrovich.

"'Wait a bit!' I answered, with a smile; I had my own views on the subject.

"A number of people had already gathered at the prince's hut. It is the custom of the Asiatics, you know, to invite all and sundry to a wedding. We were received with every mark of honor and conducted to the guest-chamber. All the same, I did not forget quietly to mark where our horses were put, in case anything unforeseen should happen."

8

"How are weddings celebrated amongst them?" I asked the staff-captain.

"Oh, in the usual way. First of all, the Mullah reads them something out of the Koran; then gifts are bestowed upon the young couple and all their relations; the next thing is eating and drinking of buza, then the dance on horseback; and there is always some ragamuffin, bedaubed with grease, bestriding a wretched, lame jade, and grimacing, buffooning, and making the worshipful company laugh. Finally, when darkness falls, they proceed to hold what we should call a ball in the guest-chamber. A poor, old greybeard strums on a three-stringed instrument—I forget what they call it, but anyhow, it is something in the nature of our balalaika. [8] The girls and young children set themselves in two ranks, one opposite the other, and clap their hands and sing. Then a girl and a man come out into the center and begin to chant verses to each other—whatever comes into their heads—and the rest join in as a chorus. Pechorin and I sat in the place of honor. All at once up came our host's youngest daughter, a girl of about sixteen, and chanted to Pechorin—how shall I put it?—something in the nature of a compliment."...

"What was it she sang—do you remember?"

"It went like this, I fancy: 'Handsome, they say, are our young horsemen, and the tunics they wear are garnished with silver; but handsomer still is the young Russian officer, and the lace on his tunic is wrought of gold. Like a poplar amongst them he stands, but in gardens of ours such trees will grow not nor bloom!'

"Pechorin rose, bowed to her, put his hand to his forehead and heart, and asked me to answer her. I know their language well, and I translated his reply.

"When she had left us I whispered to Grigori Aleksandrovich:

"'Well, now, what do you think of her?'

"'Charming!' he replied. 'What is her name?'

"'Her name is Bela,' I answered.

"And a beautiful girl she was indeed; her figure was tall and slender, her eyes black as those of a mountain chamois, and they fairly looked into your soul. Pechorin, deep in thought, kept his gaze fixed upon her, and she, for her part, stole glances at him often enough from under her lashes. Pechorin, however, was not the only one who was admiring the pretty princess; another pair of eyes, fixed and fiery, were gazing at her from the

---

[8] A kind of two-stringed or three-stringed guitar.

corner of the room. I took a good look at their owner, and recognized my old acquaintance Kazbich, who, you must know, was neither exactly 'friendly' nor yet the other thing. He was an object of much suspicion, although he had never actually been caught at any knavery. He used to bring rams to our fortress and sell them cheaply; only he never would haggle; whatever he demanded at first you had to give. He would have his throat cut rather than come down in price. He had the reputation of being fond of roaming on the far side of the Kuban with the Abreks; and, to tell the truth, he had a regular thief's visage. A little, wizened, broad-shouldered fellow he was—but smart, I can tell you, smart as the very devil! His tunic was always worn out and patched, but his weapons were mounted in silver. His horse was renowned throughout Kabardia—and, indeed, a better one it would be impossible to imagine! Not without good reason did all the other horsemen envy Kazbich, and on more than one occasion they had attempted to steal the horse, but they had never succeeded. I seem to see the animal before me now—black as coal, with legs like bow-strings and eyes as fine as Bela's! How strong he was too! He would gallop as much as fifty versts at a stretch! And he was well trained besides—he would trot behind his master like a dog, and actually knew his voice! Kazbich never used to tether him either—just the very horse for a robber!...

"On that evening Kazbich was more sullen than ever, and I noticed that he was wearing a coat of mail under his tunic. 'He hasn't got that coat of mail on for nothing,' I thought. 'He has some plot in his head, I'll be bound!'

"It grew oppressively hot in the hut, and I went out into the air to cool myself. Night had fallen upon the mountains, and a mist was beginning to creep along the gorges.

"It occurred to me to pop in under the shed where our horses were standing, to see whether they had their fodder; and, besides, it is never any harm to take precautions. My horse was a splendid one too, and more than one Kabardian had already cast fond glances at it, repeating at the same time: 'Yakshi tkhe chok yakshi.' [9]

"I stole along the fence. Suddenly I heard voices, one of which I immediately recognized.

"It was that of the young pickle, Azamat, our host's son. The other person spoke less and in a quieter tone.

"'What are they discussing there?' I wondered. 'Surely it can't be my horse!' I squatted down beside the fence and proceeded to play the eavesdropper, trying not to let slip a single word. At times the noise of songs and the buzz

---

[9] "Good—very good."

of voices, escaping from the hut, drowned the conversation which I was finding interesting.

"'That's a splendid horse of yours,' Azamat was saying. 'If I were master of a house of my own and had a stud of three hundred mares, I would give half of it for your galloper, Kazbich!'

"'Aha! Kazbich!' I said to myself, and I called to mind the coat of mail.

"'Yes,' replied Kazbich, after an interval of silence. 'There is not such another to be found in all Kabardia. Once—it was on the other side of the Terek—I had ridden with the Abreks to seize the Russian herds. We had no luck, so we scattered in different directions. Four Cossacks dashed after me. I could actually hear the cries of the giaours behind me, and in front of me there was a dense forest. I crouched down in the saddle, committed myself to Allah, and, for the first time in my life, insulted my horse with a blow of the whip. Like a bird, he plunged among the branches; the sharp thorns tore my clothing, the dead boughs of the cork-elms struck against my face! My horse leaped over tree-trunks and burst his way through bushes with his chest! It would have been better for me to have abandoned him at the outskirts of the forest and concealed myself in it afoot, but it was a pity to part with him—and the Prophet rewarded me. A few bullets whistled over my head. I could now hear the Cossacks, who had dismounted, running upon my tracks. Suddenly a deep gully opened before me. My galloper took thought—and leaped. His hind hoofs slipped back off the opposite bank, and he remained hanging by his fore-feet. I dropped the bridle and threw myself into the hollow, thereby saving my horse, which jumped out. The Cossacks saw the whole scene, only not one of them got down to search for me, thinking probably that I had mortally injured myself; and I heard them rushing to catch my horse. My heart bled within me. I crept along the hollow through the thick grass—then I looked around: it was the end of the forest. A few Cossacks were riding out from it on to the clearing, and there was my Karagyoz [10] galloping straight towards them. With a shout they all dashed forward. For a long, long time they pursued him, and one of them, in particular, was once or twice almost successful in throwing a lasso over his neck.

"I trembled, dropped my eyes, and began to pray. After a few moments I looked up again, and there was my Karagyoz flying along, his tail waving—free as the wind; and the giaours, on their jaded horses, were trailing along far behind, one after another, across the steppe. Wallah! It is true—really true! Till late at night I lay in the hollow. Suddenly—what do you think, Azamat? I heard in the darkness a horse trotting along the bank of the hollow, snorting, neighing, and beating the ground with his hoofs. I

---

[10] Turkish for "Black-eye."

11

recognized my Karagyoz's voice; 'twas he, my comrade!"... Since that time we have never been parted!'

"And I could hear him patting his galloper's sleek neck with his hand, as he called him various fond names.

"'If I had a stud of a thousand mares,' said Azamat, 'I would give it all for your Karagyoz!'

"'Yok! [11] I would not take it!' said Kazbich indifferently.

"'Listen, Kazbich,' said Azamat, trying to ingratiate himself with him. 'You are a kindhearted man, you are a brave horseman, but my father is afraid of the Russians and will not allow me to go on the mountains. Give me your horse, and I will do anything you wish. I will steal my father's best rifle for you, or his sabre—just as you like—and his sabre is a genuine Gurda; [12] you have only to lay the edge against your hand, and it will cut you; a coat of mail like yours is nothing against it.'

"Kazbich remained silent.

"'The first time I saw your horse,' continued Azamat, 'when he was wheeling and leaping under you, his nostrils distended, and the flints flying in showers from under his hoofs, something I could not understand took place within my soul; and since that time I have been weary of everything. I have looked with disdain on my father's best gallopers; I have been ashamed to be seen on them, and yearning has taken possession of me. In my anguish I have spent whole days on the cliffs, and, every minute, my thoughts have kept turning to your black galloper with his graceful gait and his sleek back, straight as an arrow. With his keen, bright eyes he has looked into mine as if about to speak!... I shall die, Kazbich, if you will not sell him to me!' said Azamat, with trembling voice.

"I could hear him burst out weeping, and I must tell you that Azamat was a very stubborn lad, and that not for anything could tears be wrung from him, even when he was a little younger.

"In answer to his tears, I could hear something like a laugh.

"'Listen,' said Azamat in a firm voice. 'You see, I am making up my mind for anything. If you like, I will steal my sister for you! How she dances! How she sings! And the way she embroiders with gold—marvelous! Not even a Turkish Padishah [13] has had a wife like her!... Shall I? Wait for me

---

[11] "No!"

[12] A particular kind of ancient and valued sabre.

[13] King—a title of the Sultan of Turkey.

12

to-morrow night, yonder, in the gorge where the torrent flows; I will go by with her to the neighboring village—and she is yours. Surely Bela is worth your galloper!'

"Kazbich remained silent for a long, long time. At length, instead of answering, he struck up in an undertone the ancient song:

"Many a beauty among us dwells

From whose eyes' dark depths the starlight wells,

'Tis an envied lot and sweet, to hold

Their love; but brighter is freedom bold.

Four wives are yours if you pay the gold;

But a mettlesome steed is of price untold;

The whirlwind itself on the steppe is less fleet;

He knows no treachery—no deceit." [14]

"In vain Azamat entreated him to consent. He wept, coaxed, and swore to him. Finally, Kazbich interrupted him impatiently:

"'Begone, you crazy brat! How should you think to ride on my horse? In three steps you would be thrown and your neck broken on the stones!'

"'I?' cried Azamat in a fury, and the blade of the child's dagger rang against the coat of mail. A powerful arm thrust him away, and he struck the wattle fence with such violence that it rocked.

"'Now we'll see some fun!' I thought to myself.

"I rushed into the stable, bridled our horses and led them out into the back courtyard. In a couple of minutes there was a terrible uproar in the hut. What had happened was this: Azamat had rushed in, with his tunic torn, saying that Kazbich was going to murder him. All sprang out, seized their guns, and the fun began! Noise—shouts—shots! But by this time Kazbich was in the saddle, and, wheeling among the crowd along the street, defended himself like a madman, brandishing his sabre.

"'It is a bad thing to interfere in other people's quarrels,' I said to Grigori

---

[14] I beg my readers' pardon for having versified Kazbich's song, which, of course, as I heard it, was in prose; but habit is second nature.

Aleksandrovich, taking him by the arm. 'Wouldn't it be better for us to clear off without loss of time?'

"'Wait, though, and see how it will end!'

"'Oh, as to that, it will be sure enough to end badly; it is always so with these Asiatics. Once let them get drunk on buza, and there's certain to be bloodshed.'

"We mounted and galloped home."


# CHAPTER IV


"TELL me, what became of Kazbich?" I asked the staff-captain impatiently.

"Why, what can happen to that sort of a fellow?" he answered, finishing his tumbler of tea. "He slipped away, of course."

"And wasn't he wounded?" I asked.

"Goodness only knows! Those scoundrels take a lot of killing! In action, for instance, I've seen many a one, sir, stuck all over with bayonets like a sieve, and still brandishing his sabre."

After an interval of silence the staff-captain continued, tapping the ground with his foot:

"One thing I'll never forgive myself for. On our arrival at the fortress the devil put it into my head to repeat to Grigori Aleksandrovich all that I had heard when I was eavesdropping behind the fence. He laughed—cunning fellow!—and thought out a little plan of his own."

"What was that? Tell me, please."

"Well, there's no help for it now, I suppose. I've begun the story, and so I must continue.

"In about four days' time Azamat rode over to the fortress. As his usual custom was, he went to see Grigori Aleksandrovich, who always used to give him sweetmeats to eat. I was present. The conversation was on the subject of horses, and Pechorin began to sound the praises of Kazbich's

Karagyoz. What a mettlesome horse it was, and how handsome! A perfect chamois! In fact, judging by his account, there simply wasn't another like it in the whole world!

"The young Tartar's beady eyes began to sparkle, but Pechorin didn't seem to notice the fact. I started to talk about something else, but immediately, mark you, Pechorin caused the conversation to strike off on to Kazbich's horse. Every time that Azamat came it was the same story. After about three weeks, I began to observe that Azamat was growing pale and wasted, just as people in novels do from love, sir. What wonder either!...

"Well, you see, it was not until afterwards that I learned the whole trick— Grigori Aleksandrovich exasperated Azamat to such an extent with his teasing that the boy was ready even to drown himself. One day Pechorin suddenly broke out with:

"'I see, Azamat, that you have taken a desperate fancy to that horse of Kazbich's, but you'll no more see him than you will the back of your neck! Come, tell me, what would you give if somebody made you a present of him?'

"'Anything he wanted,' answered Azamat.

"'In that case I will get the horse for you, only on one condition... Swear that you will fulfill  it?'

"'I swear. You swear too!'

"'Very well! I swear that the horse shall be yours. But, in return, you must deliver your sister Bela into my hands. Karagyoz shall be her bridegroom's gift. I hope the transaction will be a profitable one for you.'

"Azamat remained silent.

"'Won't you? Well, just as you like! I thought you were a man, but it seems you are still a child; it is early for you to be riding on horseback!'

"Azamat fired up.

"'But my father—' he said.

"'Does he never go away, then?'

"'True.'

"'You agree?'

"'I agree,' whispered Azamat, pale as death. 'But when?'

"'The first time Kazbich rides over here. He has promised to drive in half a score of rams; the rest is my affair. Look out, then, Azamat!'

"And so they settled the business—a bad business, to tell the truth! I said as much to Pechorin afterwards, but he only answered that a wild Circassian girl ought to consider herself fortunate in having such a charming husband as himself—because, according to their ideas, he really was her husband—and that Kazbich was a scoundrel, and ought to be punished. Judge for yourself, what could I say to that?... At the time, however, I knew nothing of their conspiracy. Well, one day Kazbich rode up and asked whether we needed any rams and honey; and I ordered him to bring some the next day.

"'Azamat!' said Grigori Aleksandrovich; 'to-morrow Karagyoz will be in my hands; if Bela is not here to-night you will never see the horse.'..

"'Very well,' said Azamat, and galloped to the village.

"In the evening Grigori Aleksandrovich armed himself and rode out of the fortress. How they settled the business I don't know, but at night they both returned, and the sentry saw that across Azamat's saddle a woman was lying, bound hand and foot and with her head wrapped in a veil."

"And the horse?" I asked the staff-captain.

"One minute! One minute! Early next morning Kazbich rode over, driving in half a score of rams for sale. Tethering his horse by the fence, he came in to see me, and I regaled him with tea, for, robber though he was, he was none the less my guest-friend.

"We began to chat about one thing and another... Suddenly I saw Kazbich start, change countenance, and dart to the window; but unfortunately the window looked on to the back courtyard.

"'What is the matter with you?' I asked.

"'My horse!... My horse!' he cried, all of a tremble.

"As a matter of fact I heard the clattering of hoofs.

"'It is probably some Cossack who has ridden up.'

"'No! Urus—yaman, yaman!' [15] he roared, and rushed headlong away like a

---

[15] "No! Russian—bad, bad!"

wild panther. In two bounds he was in the courtyard; at the gate of the fortress the sentry barred the way with his gun; Kazbich jumped over the gun and dashed off at a run along the road... Dust was whirling in the distance—Azamat was galloping away on the mettlesome Karagyoz. Kazbich, as he ran, tore his gun out of its cover and fired. For a moment he remained motionless, until he had assured himself that he had missed. Then he uttered a shrill cry, knocked the gun against a rock, smashed it to splinters, fell to the ground, and burst out sobbing like a child... The people from the fortress gathered round him, but he took no notice of anyone. They stood there talking awhile and then went back. I ordered the money for the rams to be placed beside him. He didn't touch it, but lay with his face to the ground like a dead man. Would you believe it? He remained lying like that throughout the rest of that day and the following night! It was only on the next morning that he came to the fortress and proceeded to ask that the name of the thief should be told him. The sentry who had observed Azamat untying the horse and galloping away on him did not see any necessity for concealment. At the name of Azamat, Kazbich's eyes flashed, and he set off to the village where Azamat's father lived." ..."And what about the father?"

"Ah, that was where the trick came in! Kazbich could not find him; he had gone away somewhere for five or six days; otherwise, how could Azamat have succeeded in carrying off Bela?

"And, when the father returned, there was neither daughter nor son to be found. A wily rogue, Azamat! He understood, you see, that he would lose his life if he was caught. So, from that time, he was never seen again; probably he joined some gang of Abreks and laid down his turbulent life on the other side of the Terek or the Kuban. It would have served him right!"...

# CHAPTER V

"I CONFESS that, for my part, I had trouble enough over the business. So soon as ever I learned that the Circassian girl was with Grigori Aleksandrovich, I put on my epaulettes and sword and went to see him.

"He was lying on the bed in the outer room, with one hand under his head and the other holding a pipe which had gone out. The door leading to the inner room was locked, and there was no key in the lock. I observed all that in a moment... I coughed and rapped my heels against the threshold, but he pretended not to hear.

"'Ensign!' I said, as sternly as I could. 'Do you not see that I have come to you?'

"'Ah, good morning, Maksim Maksimych! Won't you have a pipe?' he answered, without rising.

"'Excuse me, I am not Maksim Maksimych. I am the staff-captain.'

"'It's all the same! Won't you have some tea? If you only knew how I am being tortured with anxiety.'

"'I know all,' I answered, going up to the bed.

"'So much the better,' he said. 'I am not in a narrative mood.'

"'Ensign, you have committed an offence for which I may have to answer as well as you.'

"'Oh, that'll do. What's the harm? You know, we've gone halves in everything.'

"'What sort of a joke do you think you are playing? Your sword, please!'...

"'Mitka, my sword!'

"'Mitka brought the sword. My duty discharged, I sat down on the bed, facing Pechorin, and said: 'Listen here, Grigori Aleksandrovich, you must admit that this is a bad business.'

"'What is?'

"'Why, that you have carried off Bela... Ah, it is that beast Azamat!... Come, confess!' I said.

"'But, supposing I am fond of her?'...

"Well, what could I say to that?... I was nonplussed. After a short interval of silence, however, I told him that if Bela's father were to claim her he would have to give her up.

"'Not at all!'

"'But he will get to know that she is here.'

"'How?'

"Again I was nonplussed.

18

"'Listen, Maksim Maksimych,' said Pechorin, rising to his feet. 'You're a kind-hearted man, you know; but, if we give that savage back his daughter, he will cut her throat or sell her. The deed is done, and the only thing we can do now is not to go out of our way to spoil matters. Leave Bela with me and keep my sword!'

"'Show her to me, though,' I said.

"'She is behind that door. Only I wanted, myself, to see her to-day and wasn't able to. She sits in the corner, muffled in her veil, and neither speaks nor looks up—timid as a wild chamois! I have hired the wife of our dukhan-keeper: she knows the Tartar language, and will look after Bela and accustom her to the idea that she belongs to me—for she shall belong to no one else!' he added, banging his fist on the table.

"I assented to that too... What could I do? There are some people with whom you absolutely have to agree."

"Well?" I asked Maksim Maksimych. "Did he really succeed in making her grow accustomed to him, or did she pine away in captivity from home-sickness?"

"Good gracious! how could she pine away from home-sickness? From the fortress she could see the very same hills as she could from the village—and these savages require nothing more. Besides, Grigori Aleksandrovich used to give her a present of some kind every day. At first she didn't utter a word, but haughtily thrust away the gifts, which then fell to the lot of the dukhan-keeper's wife and aroused her eloquence. Ah, presents! What won't a woman do for a colored rag!... But that is by the way... For a long time Grigori Aleksandrovich persevered with her, and meanwhile he studied the Tartar language and she began to understand ours. Little by little she grew accustomed to looking at him, at first furtively, askance; but she still pined and crooned her songs in an undertone, so that even I would feel heavy at heart when I heard her from the next room. One scene I shall never forget: I was walking past, and I looked in at the window; Bela was sitting on the stove-couch, her head sunk on her breast, and Grigori Aleksandrovich was standing, facing her.

"'Listen, my Peri,' he was saying. 'Surely you know that you will have to be mine sooner or later—why, then, do you but torture me? Is it that you are in love with some Chechene? If so, I will let you go home at once.'

"She gave a scarcely perceptible start and shook her head.

"'Or is it,' he continued, 'that I am utterly hateful to you?'

"She heaved a sigh.

19

"'Or that your faith prohibits you from giving me a little of your love?'

"She turned pale and remained silent.

"'Believe me, Allah is one and the same for all races; and, if he permits me to love you, why, then, should he prohibit you from requiting me by returning my love?'

"She gazed fixedly into his face, as though struck by that new idea. Distrust and a desire to be convinced were expressed in her eyes. What eyes they were! They sparkled just like two glowing coals.

"'Listen, my dear, good Bela!' continued Pechorin. 'You see how I love you. I am ready to give up everything to make you cheerful once more. I want you to be happy, and, if you are going to be sad again, I shall die. Tell me, you will be more cheerful?'

"She fell into thought, her black eyes still fixed upon him. Then she smiled graciously and nodded her head in token of acquiescence.

"He took her by the hand and tried to induce her to kiss him. She defended herself feebly, and only repeated: 'Please! Please! You mustn't, you mustn't!'

"He went on to insist; she began to tremble and weep.

"'I am your captive,' she said, 'your slave; of course, you can compel me.'

"And then, again—tears.

"Grigori Aleksandrovich struck his forehead with his fist and sprang into the other room. I went in to see him, and found him walking moodily backwards and forwards with folded arms.

"'Well, old man?' I said to him.

"'She is a devil—not a woman!' he answered. 'But I give you my word of honor that she shall be mine!'

"I shook my head.

"'Will you bet with me?' he said. 'In a week's time?'

"'Very well,' I answered.

"We shook hands on it and separated.

"The next day he immediately despatched an express messenger to Kizlyar to purchase some things for him. The messenger brought back a quite innumerable quantity of various Persian stuffs.

"'What think you, Maksim Maksimych?' he said to me, showing the presents. 'Will our Asiatic beauty hold out against such a battery as this?'

"'You don't know the Circassian women,' I answered. 'They are not at all the same as the Georgian or the Transcaucasian Tartar women—not at all! They have their own principles, they are brought up differently.'

"Grigori Aleksandrovich smiled and began to whistle a march to himself."

# CHAPTER VI

"AS things fell out, however," continued Maksim Maksimych, "I was right, you see. The presents produced only half an effect. She became more gracious more trustful—but that was all. Pechorin accordingly determined upon a last expedient. One morning he ordered his horse to be saddled, dressed himself as a Circassian, armed himself, and went into her room.

"'Bela,' he said. 'You know how I love you. I decided to carry you off, thinking that when you grew to know me you would give me your love. I was mistaken. Farewell! Remain absolute mistress of all I possess. Return to your father if you like—you are free. I have acted wrongfully towards you, and I must punish myself. Farewell! I am going. Whither?—How should I know? Perchance I shall not have long to court the bullet or the sabre-stroke. Then remember me and forgive.'

"He turned away, and stretched out his hand to her in farewell. She did not take his hand, but remained silent. But I, standing there behind the door, was able through a chink to observe her countenance, and I felt sorry for her—such a deathly pallor shrouded that charming little face! Hearing no answer, Pechorin took a few steps towards the door. He was trembling, and—shall I tell you?—I think that he was in a state to perform in very fact what he had been saying in jest! He was just that sort of man, Heaven knows!

"He had scarcely touched the door, however, when Bela sprang to her feet, burst out sobbing, and threw herself on his neck! Would you believe it? I, standing there behind the door, fell to weeping too, that is to say, you know, not exactly weeping—but just—well, something foolish!"

The staff-captain became silent.

"Yes, I confess," he said after a while, tugging at his moustache, "I felt hurt that not one woman had ever loved me like that."

"Was their happiness lasting?" I asked.

"Yes, she admitted that, from the day she had first cast eyes on Pechorin, she had often dreamed of him, and that no other man had ever produced such an impression upon her. Yes, they were happy!"

"How tiresome!" I exclaimed, involuntarily.

In point of fact, I had been expecting a tragic ending—when, lo! he must needs disappoint my hopes in such an unexpected manner!...

"Is it possible, though," I continued, "that her father did not guess that she was with you in the fortress?"

"Well, you must know, he seems to have had his suspicions. After a few days, we learned that the old man had been murdered. This is how it happened."...

My attention was aroused anew.

"I must tell you that Kazbich imagined that the horse had been stolen by Azamat with his father's consent; at any rate, that is what I suppose. So, one day, Kazbich went and waited by the roadside, about three versts beyond the village. The old man was returning from one of his futile searches for his daughter; his retainers were lagging behind. It was dusk. Deep in thought, he was riding at a walking pace when, suddenly, Kazbich darted out like a cat from behind a bush, sprang up behind him on the horse, flung him to the ground with a thrust of his dagger, seized the bridle and was off. A few of the retainers saw the whole affair from the hill; they dashed off in pursuit of Kazbich, but failed to overtake him."

"He requited himself for the loss of his horse, and took his revenge at the same time," I said, with a view to evoking my companion's opinion.

"Of course, from their point of view," said the staff-captain, "he was perfectly right."

I was involuntarily struck by the aptitude which the Russian displays for accommodating himself to the customs of the people in whose midst he happens to be living. I know not whether this mental quality is deserving of censure or commendation, but it proves the incredible pliancy of his mind and the presence of that clear common sense which pardons evil wherever it sees that evil is inevitable or impossible of annihilation.

22

# CHAPTER VII

IN the meantime we had finished our tea. The horses, which had been put to long before, were freezing in the snow. In the west the moon was growing pale, and was just on the point of plunging into the black clouds which were hanging over the distant summits like the shreds of a torn curtain. We went out of the hut. Contrary to my fellow-traveller's prediction, the weather had cleared up, and there was a promise of a calm morning. The dancing choirs of the stars were interwoven in wondrous patterns on the distant horizon, and, one after another, they flickered out as the wan resplendence of the east suffused the dark, lilac vault of heaven, gradually illumining the steep mountain slopes, covered with the virgin snows. To right and left loomed grim and mysterious chasms, and masses of mist, eddying and coiling like snakes, were creeping thither along the furrows of the neighboring cliffs, as though sentient and fearful of the approach of day.

All was calm in heaven and on earth, calm as within the heart of a man at the moment of morning-prayer; only at intervals a cool wind rushed in from the east, lifting the horses' manes which were covered with hoar-frost. We started off. The five lean jades dragged our wagons with difficulty along the tortuous road up Mount Get. We ourselves walked behind, placing stones under the wheels whenever the horses were spent. The road seemed to lead into the sky, for, so far as the eye could discern, it still mounted up and up, until finally it was lost in the cloud which, since early evening, had been resting on the summit of Mount Get, like a kite awaiting its prey. The snow crunched under our feet. The atmosphere grew so rarefied that to breathe was painful; ever and anon the blood rushed to my head, but withal a certain rapturous sensation was diffused throughout my veins and I felt a species of delight at being so high up above the world. A childish feeling, I admit, but, when we retire from the conventions of society and draw close to nature, we involuntarily become as children: each attribute acquired by experience falls away from the soul, which becomes anew such as it was once and will surely be again. He whose lot it has been, as mine has been, to wander over the desolate mountains, long, long to observe their fantastic shapes, greedily to gulp down the life-giving air diffused through their ravines—he, of course, will understand my desire to communicate, to narrate, to sketch those magic pictures.

Well, at length we reached the summit of Mount Gut and, halting, looked around us. Upon the mountain a grey cloud was hanging, and its cold breath threatened the approach of a storm; but in the east everything was so clear and golden that we—that is, the staff-captain and I—forgot all about the cloud... Yes, the staff-captain too; in simple hearts the feeling for

23

the beauty and grandeur of nature is a hundred-fold stronger and more vivid than in us, ecstatic composers of narratives in words and on paper.

"You have grown accustomed, I suppose, to these magnificent pictures!" I said.

"Yes, sir, you can even grow accustomed to the whistling of a bullet, that is to say, accustomed to concealing the involuntary thumping of your heart."

"I have heard, on the contrary, that many an old warrior actually finds that music agreeable."

"Of course, if it comes to that, it is agreeable; but only just because the heart beats more violently. Look!" he added, pointing towards the east. "What a country!"

And, indeed, such a panorama I can hardly hope to see elsewhere. Beneath us lay the Koishaur Valley, intersected by the Aragva and another stream as if by two silver threads; a bluish mist was gliding along the valley, fleeing into the neighboring defiles from the warm rays of the morning. To right and left the mountain crests, towering higher and higher, intersected each other and stretched out, covered with snows and thickets; in the distance were the same mountains, which now, however, had the appearance of two cliffs, one like to the other. And all these snows were burning in the crimson glow so merrily and so brightly that it seemed as though one could live in such a place for ever. The sun was scarcely visible behind the dark-blue mountain, which only a practiced eye could distinguish from a thunder-cloud; but above the sun was a blood-red streak to which my companion directed particular attention.

"I told you," he exclaimed, "that there would be dirty weather to-day! We must make haste, or perhaps it will catch us on Mount Krestov.—Get on!" he shouted to the drivers.

Chains were put under the wheels in place of drags, so that they should not slide, the drivers took the horses by the reins, and the descent began. On the right was a cliff, on the left a precipice, so deep that an entire village of Ossetes at the bottom looked like a swallow's nest. I shuddered, as the thought occurred to me that often in the depth of night, on that very road, where two wagons could not pass, a courier drives some ten times a year without climbing down from his rickety vehicle. One of our drivers was a Russian peasant from Yaroslavl, the other, an Ossete. The latter took out the leaders in good time and led the shaft-horse by the reins, using every possible precaution—but our heedless compatriot did not even climb down from his box! When I remarked to him that he might put himself out a bit, at least in the interests of my portmanteau, for which I had not the slightest desire to clamber down into the abyss, he answered:

"Eh, master, with the help of Heaven we shall arrive as safe and sound as the others; it's not our first time, you know."

And he was right. We might just as easily have failed to arrive at all; but arrive we did, for all that. And if people would only reason a little more they would be convinced that life is not worth taking such a deal of trouble about.

Perhaps, however, you would like to know the conclusion of the story of Bela? In the first place, this is not a novel, but a collection of travelling-notes, and, consequently, I cannot make the staff-captain tell the story sooner than he actually proceeded to tell it. Therefore, you must wait a bit, or, if you like, turn over a few pages. Though I do not advise you to do the latter, because the crossing of Mount Krestov (or, as the erudite Gamba calls it, le mont St. Christophe [16] ) is worthy of your curiosity.

Well, then, we descended Mount Gut into the Chertov Valley... There's a romantic designation for you! Already you have a vision of the evil spirit's nest amid the inaccessible cliffs—but you are out of your reckoning there. The name "Chertov" is derived from the word cherta (boundary-line) and not from chort (devil), because, at one time, the valley marked the boundary of Georgia. We found it choked with snow-drifts, which reminded us rather vividly of Saratov, Tambov, and other charming localities of our fatherland.

"Look, there is Krestov!" said the staffcaptain, when we had descended into the Chertov Valley, as he pointed out a hill covered with a shroud of snow. Upon the summit stood out the black outline of a stone cross, and past it led an all but imperceptible road which travellers use only when the side-road is obstructed with snow. Our drivers, declaring that no avalanches had yet fallen, spared the horses by conducting us round the mountain. At a turning we met four or five Ossetes, who offered us their services; and, catching hold of the wheels, proceeded, with a shout, to drag and hold up our cart. And, indeed, it is a dangerous road; on the right were masses of snow hanging above us, and ready, it seemed, at the first squall of wind to break off and drop into the ravine; the narrow road was partly covered with snow, which, in many places, gave way under our feet and, in others, was converted into ice by the action of the sun by day and the frosts by night, so that the horses kept falling, and it was with difficulty that we ourselves made our way. On the left yawned a deep chasm, through which rolled a torrent, now hiding beneath a crust of ice, now leaping and foaming over the black rocks. In two hours we were barely able to double Mount Krestov—two versts in two hours! Meanwhile the clouds had descended, hail and snow fell; the wind, bursting into the ravines, howled

---

[16] Krestov is an adjective meaning "of the cross" (Krest=cross); and, of course, is not the Russian for "Christophe."

and whistled like Nightingale the Robber. [17] Soon the stone cross was hidden in the mist, the billows of which, in ever denser and more compact masses, rushed in from the east...

Concerning that stone cross, by the way, there exists the strange, but widespread, tradition that it had been set up by the Emperor Peter the First when travelling through the Caucasus. In the first place, however, the Emperor went no farther than Daghestan; and, in the second place, there is an inscription in large letters on the cross itself, to the effect that it had been erected by order of General Ermolov, and that too in the year 1824. Nevertheless, the tradition has taken such firm root, in spite of the inscription, that really you do not know what to believe; the more so, as it is not the custom to believe inscriptions.

To reach the station Kobi, we still had to descend about five versts, across ice-covered rocks and plashy snow. The horses were exhausted; we were freezing; the snowstorm droned with ever-increasing violence, exactly like the storms of our own northern land, only its wild melodies were sadder and more melancholy.

"O Exile," I thought, "thou art weeping for thy wide, free steppes! There mayest thou unfold thy cold wings, but here thou art stifled and confined, like an eagle beating his wings, with a shriek, against the grating of his iron cage!"

"A bad look out," said the staff-captain. "Look! There's nothing to be seen all round but mist and snow. At any moment we may tumble into an abyss or stick fast in a cleft; and a little lower down, I dare say, the Baidara has risen so high that there is no getting across it. Oh, this Asia, I know it! Like people, like rivers! There's no trusting them at all!"

The drivers, shouting and cursing, belabored the horses, which snorted, resisted obstinately, and refused to budge on any account, notwithstanding the eloquence of the whips.

"Your honor," one of the drivers said to me at length, "you see, we will never reach Kobi to-day. Won't you give orders to turn to the left while we can? There is something black yonder on the slope—probably huts. Travellers always stop there in bad weather, sir. They say," he added, pointing to the Ossetes, "that they will lead us there if you will give them a tip."

"I know that, my friend, I know that without your telling me," said the staff-captain. "Oh, these beasts! They are delighted to seize any pretext for extorting a tip!"

---

[17] A legendary Russian hero whose whistling knocked people down.

26

"You must confess, however," I said, "that we should be worse off without them."

"Just so, just so," he growled to himself. "I know them well—these guides! They scent out by instinct a chance of taking advantage of people. As if it was impossible to find the way without them!"

Accordingly we turned aside to the left, and, somehow or other, after a good deal of trouble, made our way to the wretched shelter, which consisted of two huts built of stone slabs and rubble, surrounded by a wall of the same material. Our ragged hosts received us with alacrity. I learned afterwards that the Government supplies them with money and food upon condition that they put up travellers who are overtaken by storm.

# CHAPTER VIII

"ALL is for the best," I said, sitting down close by the fire. "Now you will finish telling me your story about Bela. I am certain that what you have already told me was not the end of it."

"Why are you so certain?" answered the staff-captain, winking and smiling slyly.

"Because things don't happen like that. A story with such an unusual beginning must also have an unusual ending."

"You have guessed, of course"...

"I am very glad to hear it."

"It is all very well for you to be glad, but, indeed, it makes me sad when I think of it. Bela was a splendid girl. In the end I grew accustomed to her just as if she had been my own daughter, and she loved me. I must tell you that I have no family. I have had no news of my father and mother for twelve years or so, and, in my earlier days, I never thought of providing myself with a wife—and now, you know, it wouldn't do. So I was glad to have found someone to spoil. She used to sing to us or dance the Lezginka.[18] And what a dancer she was! I have seen our own ladies in provincial society; and on one occasion, sir, about twenty years ago, I was

---

[18] Lezghian dance.

even in the Nobles' Club at Moscow—but was there a woman to be compared with her? Not one! Grigori Aleksandrovich dressed her up like a doll, petted and pampered her, and it was simply astonishing to see how pretty she grew while she lived with us. The sunburn disappeared from her face and hands, and a rosy color came into her cheeks... What a merry girl she was! Always making fun of me, the little rogue!... Heaven forgive her!"

"And when you told her of her father's death?"

"We kept it a secret from her for a long time, until she had grown accustomed to her position; and then, when she was told, she cried for a day or two and forgot all about it.

"For four months or so everything went on as well as it possibly could. Grigori Aleksandrovich, as I think I have already mentioned, was passionately fond of hunting; he was always craving to be off into the forest after boars or wild goats—but now it would be as much as he would do to go beyond the fortress rampart. All at once, however, I saw that he was beginning again to have fits of abstraction, walking about his room with his hands clasped behind his back. One day after that, without telling anyone, he set off shooting. During the whole morning he was not to be seen; then the same thing happened another time, and so on—oftener and oftener...

"'This looks bad!' I said to myself. 'Something must have come between them!'

"One morning I paid them a visit—I can see it all in my mind's eye, as if it was happening now. Bela was sitting on the bed, wearing a black silk jacket, and looking rather pale and so sad that I was alarmed.

"'Where is Pechorin?' I asked.

"'Hunting.'

"'When did he go—to-day?'

"'She was silent, as if she found a difficulty in answering.

"'No, he has been gone since yesterday,' she said at length, with a heavy sigh.

"'Surely nothing has happened to him!'

"'Yesterday I thought and thought the whole day,' she answered through her tears; 'I imagined all sorts of misfortunes. At one time I fancied that he had been wounded by a wild boar, at another time, that he had been carried off by a Chechene into the mountains... But, now, I have come to think that he no longer loves me.'

28

"'In truth, my dear girl, you could not have imagined anything worse!'

"She burst out crying; then, proudly raising her head, she wiped away the tears and continued:

"'If he does not love me, then who prevents him sending me home? I am not putting any constraint on him. But, if things go on like this, I will go away myself—I am not a slave, I am a prince's daughter!'...

"I tried to talk her over.

"'Listen, Bela. You see it is impossible for him to stop in here with you for ever, as if he was sewn on to your petticoat. He is a young man and fond of hunting. Off he'll go, but you will find that he will come back; and, if you are going to be unhappy, you will soon make him tired of you.'

"'True, true!' she said. 'I will be merry.'

"And with a burst of laughter, she seized her tambourine, began to sing, dance, and gambol around me. But that did not last long either; she fell upon the bed again and buried her face in her hands.

"What could I do with her? You know I have never been accustomed to the society of women. I thought and thought how to cheer her up, but couldn't hit on anything. For some time both of us remained silent... A most unpleasant situation, sir!

"At length I said to her:

"'Would you like us to go and take a walk on the rampart? The weather is splendid.'

"This was in September, and indeed it was a wonderful day, bright and not too hot. The mountains could be seen as clearly as though they were but a hand's-breadth away. We went, and walked in silence to and fro along the rampart of the fortress. At length she sat down on the sward, and I sat beside her. In truth, now, it is funny to think of it all! I used to run after her just like a kind of children's nurse!

"Our fortress was situated in a lofty position, and the view from the rampart was superb. On one side, the wide clearing, seamed by a few clefts, was bounded by the forest which stretched out to the very ridge of the mountains. Here and there, on the clearing, villages were to be seen sending forth their smoke, and there were droves of horses roaming about. On the other side flowed a tiny stream, and close to its banks came the dense undergrowth which covered the flinty heights joining the principal chain of the Caucasus. We sat in a corner of the bastion, so that we could see everything on both sides. Suddenly I perceived someone on a grey horse riding out of the forest; nearer and nearer he approached until finally he stopped on the far side of the river, about a hundred fathoms from us, and began to wheel his horse round and round like one possessed. 'Strange!' I thought.

"'Look, look, Bela,' I said, 'you've got young eyes—what sort of a horseman is that? Who is it he has come to amuse?'...

"'It is Kazbich!' she exclaimed after a glance.

"'Ah, the robber! Come to laugh at us, has he?'

"I looked closely, and sure enough it was Kazbich, with his swarthy face, and as ragged and dirty as ever.

"'It is my father's horse!' said Bela, seizing my arm.

"She was trembling like a leaf and her eyes were sparkling.

"'Aha!' I said to myself. 'There is robber's blood in your veins still, my dear!'

"'Come here,' I said to the sentry. 'Look to your gun and unhorse that gallant for me—and you shall have a silver ruble.'

"'Very well, your honor, only he won't keep still.'

"'Tell him to!' I said, with a laugh.

"'Hey, friend!' cried the sentry, waving his hand. 'Wait a bit. What are you spinning round like a humming-top for?'

"Kazbich halted and gave ear to the sentry—probably thinking that we were going to parley with him. Quite the contrary!... My grenadier took aim... Bang!... Missed!... Just as the powder flashed in the pan Kazbich jogged his horse, which gave a bound to one side. He stood up in his stirrups, shouted something in his own language, made a threatening gesture with his whip—and was off.

"'Aren't you ashamed of yourself?' I said to the sentry.

"'He has gone away to die, your honor,' he answered. 'There's no killing a man of that cursed race at one stroke.'

"A quarter of an hour later Pechorin returned from hunting. Bela threw herself on his neck without a single complaint, without a single reproach for his lengthy absence!... Even I was angry with him by this time!

"'Good heavens!' I said; 'why, I tell you, Kazbich was here on the other side of the river just a moment ago, and we shot at him. How easily you might have run up against him, you know! These mountaineers are a vindictive race! Do you suppose he does not guess that you gave Azamat some help? And I wager that he recognized Bela to-day! I know he was desperately fond of her a year ago—he told me so himself—and, if he had had any hope of getting together a proper bridegroom's gift, he would certainly have sought her in marriage.'

"At this Pechorin became thoughtful.

"'Yes,' he answered. 'We must be more cautious—Bela, from this day forth you mustn't walk on the rampart anymore.'

"In the evening I had a lengthy explanation with him. I was vexed that his feelings towards the poor girl had changed; to say nothing of his spending half the day hunting, his manner towards her had become cold. He rarely caressed her, and she was beginning perceptibly to pine away; her little face was becoming drawn, her large eyes growing dim.

"'What are you sighing for, Bela?' I would ask her. 'Are you sad?'

"'No!'

"'Do you want anything?'

"'No!'

"'You are pining for your kinsfolk?'

"'I have none!'

"Sometimes for whole days not a word could be drawn from her but 'Yes' and 'No.'

"So I straightway proceeded to talk to Pechorin about her."


# CHAPTER IX


"'LISTEN, Maksim Maksimych,' said Pechorin. 'Mine is an unfortunate disposition; whether it is the result of my upbringing or whether it is innate—I know not. I only know this, that if I am the cause of unhappiness in others I myself am no less unhappy. Of course, that is a poor consolation to them—only the fact remains that such is the case. In my early youth, from the moment I ceased to be under the guardianship of my relations, I began madly to enjoy all the pleasures which money could buy—and, of course, such pleasures became irksome to me. Then I launched out into the world of fashion—and that, too, soon palled upon me. I fell in love with fashionable beauties and was loved by them, but my imagination and egoism alone were aroused; my heart remained empty... I began to read, to study—but sciences also became utterly wearisome to me. I saw that neither fame nor happiness depends on them in the least, because the happiest people are the uneducated, and fame is good fortune, to attain which you have only to be smart. Then I grew bored... Soon afterwards I was transferred to the Caucasus; and that was the happiest time of my life. I hoped that under the bullets of the Chechenes boredom could not exist—a vain hope! In a month I grew so accustomed to the buzzing of the bullets and to the proximity of death that, to tell the truth, I paid more attention to the gnats—and I became more bored than ever, because I had lost what was almost my last hope. When I saw Bela in my own house; when, for the first time, I held her on my knee and kissed her black locks, I, fool that I was, thought that she was an angel sent to me by sympathetic fate... Again I was mistaken; the love of a savage is little better than that of your lady of quality, the barbaric ignorance and simplicity of the one weary you as much as the coquetry of the other. I am not saying that I do not love her still; I am grateful to her for a few fairly sweet moments; I would give my life for her—only I am bored with her... Whether I am a fool or a villain I know not; but this is certain, I am also most deserving of pity—perhaps more than she. My soul has been spoiled by the world, my imagination is unquiet, my heart insatiate. To me everything is of little moment. I become as easily accustomed to grief as to joy, and my life grows emptier day by day. One expedient only is left to me—travel.

"'As soon as I can, I shall set off—but not to Europe. Heaven forfend! I shall go to America, to Arabia, to India—perchance I shall die somewhere on the way. At any rate, I am convinced that, thanks to storms and bad roads, that last consolation will not quickly be exhausted!'

"For a long time he went on speaking thus, and his words have remained stamped upon my memory, because it was the first time that I had heard such things from a man of five-and-twenty—and Heaven grant it may be the last. Isn't it astonishing? Tell me, please," continued the staff-captain, appealing to me. "You used to live in the Capital, I think, and that not so very long ago. Is it possible that the young men there are all like that?"

I replied that there were a good many people who used the same sort of language, that, probably, there might even be some who spoke in all sincerity; that disillusionment, moreover, like all other vogues, having had its beginning in the higher strata of society, had descended to the lower, where it was being worn threadbare, and that, now, those who were really and truly bored strove to conceal their misfortune as if it were a vice. The staff-captain did not understand these subtleties, shook his head, and smiled slyly.

"Anyhow, I suppose it was the French who introduced the fashion?"

"No, the English."

"Aha, there you are!" he answered. "They always have been arrant drunkards, you know!"

Involuntarily I recalled to mind a certain lady, living in Moscow, who used to maintain that Byron was nothing more nor less than a drunkard. However, the staff-captain's observation was more excusable; in order to abstain from strong drink, he naturally endeavored to convince himself that all the misfortunes in the world are the result of drunkenness.

# CHAPTER X

MEANWHILE the staff-captain continued his story.

"Kazbich never put in an appearance again; but somehow—I don't know why—I could not get the idea out of my head that he had had a reason for coming, and that some mischievous scheme was in his mind.

"Well, one day Pechorin tried to persuade me to go boar-hunting with him. For a long time I refused. What novelty was a wild boar to me?

"However, off he dragged me, all the same. We took four or five soldiers and set out early in the morning. Up till ten o'clock we scurried about the reeds and the forest—there wasn't a wild beast to be found!

"'I say, oughtn't we to be going back?' I said. 'What's the use of sticking at it? It is evident enough that we have happened on an unlucky day!'

"But, in spite of heat and fatigue, Pechorin didn't like to return empty-handed... That is just the kind of man he was; whatever he set his heart on he had to have—evidently, in his childhood, he had been spoiled by an indulgent mother. At last, at midday, we discovered one of those cursed wild boars—Bang! Bang!—No good!—Off it went into the reeds. That was an unlucky day, to be sure!... So, after a short rest, we set off homeward...

"We rode in silence, side by side, giving the horses their head. We had almost reached the fortress, and only the brushwood concealed it from view. Suddenly a shot rang out... We glanced at each other, both struck with the selfsame suspicion... We galloped headlong in the direction of the shot, looked, and saw the soldiers clustered together on the rampart and pointing towards a field, along which a rider was flying at full speed, holding something white across his saddle. Grigori Aleksandrovich yelled like any Chechene, whipped his gun from its cover, and gave chase—I after him.

"Luckily, thanks to our unsuccessful hunt, our horses were not jaded; they strained under the saddle, and with every moment we drew nearer and nearer... At length I recognized Kazbich, only I could not make out what it was that he was holding in front of him.

"Then I drew level with Pechorin and shouted to him:

"'It is Kazbich!'

"He looked at me, nodded, and struck his horse with his whip.

"At last we were within gunshot of Kazbich. Whether it was that his horse was jaded or not so good as ours, I don't know, but, in spite of all his efforts, it did not get along very fast. I fancy at that moment he remembered his Karagyoz!

"I looked at Pechorin. He was taking aim as he galloped...

"'Don't shoot,' I cried. 'Save the shot! We will catch up with him as it is.'

"Oh, these young men! Always taking fire at the wrong moment! The shot rang out and the bullet broke one of the horse's hind legs. It gave a few fiery leaps forward, stumbled, and fell to its knees. Kazbich sprang off, and then we perceived that it was a woman he was holding in his arms—a woman wrapped in a veil. It was Bela—poor Bela! He shouted something to us in his own language and raised his dagger over her... Delay was useless; I fired in my turn, at haphazard. Probably the bullet struck him in the shoulder, because he dropped his hand suddenly. When the smoke cleared off, we could see the wounded horse lying on the ground and Bela beside it; but Kazbich, his gun flung away, was clambering like a cat up the cliff, through the brushwood. I should have liked to have brought him down from there—but I hadn't a charge ready. We jumped off our horses and rushed to Bela. Poor girl! She was lying motionless, and the blood was pouring in streams from her wound. The villain! If he had struck her to the heart—well and good, everything would at least have been finished there and then; but to stab her in the back like that—the scoundrel! She was unconscious. We tore the veil into strips and bound up the wound as tightly as we could. In vain Pechorin kissed her cold lips—it was impossible to bring her to.

"Pechorin mounted; I lifted Bela from the ground and somehow managed to place her before him on his saddle; he put his arm round her and we rode back.

"'Look here, Maksim Maksimych,' said Grigori Aleksandrovich, after a few moments of silence. 'We will never bring her in alive like this.'

"'True!' I said, and we put our horses to a full gallop."

# CHAPTER XI

"A CROWD was awaiting us at the fortress gate. Carefully we carried the wounded girl to Pechorin's quarters, and then we sent for the doctor. The latter was drunk, but he came, examined the wound, and announced that she could not live more than a day. He was mistaken, though."

"She recovered?" I asked the staff-captain, seizing him by the arm, and involuntarily rejoicing.

"No," he replied, "but the doctor was so far mistaken that she lived two days longer."

"Explain, though, how Kazbich made off with her!"

"It was like this: in spite of Pechorin's prohibition, she went out of the fortress and down to the river. It was a very hot day, you know, and she sat on a rock and dipped her feet in the water. Up crept Kazbich, pounced upon her, silenced her, and dragged her into the bushes. Then he sprang on his horse and made off. In the meantime she succeeded in crying out, the sentries took the alarm, fired, but wide of the mark; and thereupon we arrived on the scene."

"But what did Kazbich want to carry her off for?"

"Good gracious! Why, everyone knows these Circassians are a race of thieves; they can't keep their hands off anything that is left lying about! They may not want a thing, but they will steal it, for all that. Still, you mustn't be too hard on them. And, besides, he had been in love with her for a long time."

"And Bela died?"

"Yes, she died, but she suffered for a long time, and we were fairly knocked up with her, I can tell you. About ten o'clock in the evening she came to herself. We were sitting by her bed. As soon as ever she opened her eyes she began to call Pechorin.

"'I am here beside you, my janechka' (that is, 'my darling'), he answered, taking her by the hand.

"'I shall die,' she said.

"We began to comfort her, telling her that the doctor had promised infallibly to cure her. She shook her little head and turned to the wall—she did not want to die!...

"At night she became delirious, her head burned, at times a feverish paroxysm convulsed her whole body. She talked incoherently about her father, her brother; she yearned for the mountains, for her home... Then she spoke of Pechorin also, called him various fond names, or reproached him for having ceased to love his janechka.

"He listened to her in silence, his head sunk in his hands; but yet, during the whole time, I did not notice a single tear-drop on his lashes. I do not know whether he was actually unable to weep or was mastering himself; but for my part I have never seen anything more pitiful.

"Towards morning the delirium passed off. For an hour or so she lay motionless, pale, and so weak that it was hardly possible to observe that she was breathing. After that she grew better and began to talk: only about what, think you? Such thoughts come only to the dying!... She lamented that she was not a Christian, that in the other world her soul would never meet the soul of Grigori Aleksandrovich, and that in Paradise another woman would be his companion. The thought occurred to me to baptize her before her death. I told her my idea; she looked at me undecidedly, and for a long time was unable to utter a word. Finally she answered that she would die in the faith in which she had been born. A whole day passed thus. What a change that day made in her! Her pale cheeks fell in, her eyes grew ever so large, her lips burned. She felt a consuming heat within her, as though a red-hot blade was piercing her breast.

"The second night came on. We did not close our eyes or leave the bedside. She suffered terribly, and groaned; and directly the pain began to abate she endeavored to assure Grigori Aleksandrovich that she felt better, tried to persuade him to go to bed, kissed his hand and would not let it out of hers. Before the morning she began to feel the death agony and to toss about. She knocked the bandage off, and the blood flowed afresh. When the wound was bound up again she grew quiet for a moment and begged Pechorin to kiss her. He fell on his knees beside the bed, raised her head from the pillow, and pressed his lips to hers—which were growing cold. She threw her trembling arms closely round his neck, as if with that kiss she wished to yield up her soul to him.—No, she did well to die! Why, what would have become of her if Grigori Aleksandrovich had abandoned her? And that is what would have happened, sooner or later.

"During half the following day she was calm, silent and docile, however much the doctor tortured her with his fomentations and mixtures.

"'Good heavens!' I said to him, 'you know you said yourself that she was certain to die, so what is the good of all these preparations of yours?'

"'Even so, it is better to do all this,' he replied, 'so that I may have an easy conscience.'

"A pretty conscience, forsooth!

"After midday Bela began to suffer from thirst. We opened the windows, but it was hotter outside than in the room; we placed ice round the bed—all to no purpose. I knew that that intolerable thirst was a sign of the approaching end, and I told Pechorin so.

"'Water, water!' she said in a hoarse voice, raising herself up from the bed.

"Pechorin turned pale as a sheet, seized a glass, filled it, and gave it to her. I covered my eyes with my hands and began to say a prayer—I can't remember what... Yes, my friend, many a time have I seen people die in hospitals or on the field of battle, but this was something altogether different! Still, this one thing grieves me, I must confess: she died without even once calling me to mind. Yet I loved her, I should think, like a father!... Well, God forgive her!... And, to tell the truth, what am I that she should have remembered me when she was dying?...

"As soon as she had drunk the water, she grew easier—but in about three minutes she breathed her last! We put a looking-glass to her lips—it was undimmed!

"I led Pechorin from the room, and we went on to the fortress rampart. For a long time we walked side by side, to and fro, speaking not a word and with our hands clasped behind our backs. His face expressed nothing out of the common—and that vexed me. Had I been in his place, I should have died of grief. At length he sat down on the ground in the shade and began to draw something in the sand with his stick. More for form's sake than anything, you know, I tried to console him and began to talk. He raised his head and burst into a laugh! At that laugh a cold shudder ran through me... I went away to order a coffin.

"I confess it was partly to distract my thoughts that I busied myself in that way. I possessed a little piece of Circassian stuff, and I covered the coffin with it, and decked it with some Circassian silver lace which Grigori Aleksandrovich had bought for Bela herself.

"Early next morning we buried her behind the fortress, by the river, beside the spot where she had sat for the last time. Around her little grave white acacia shrubs and elder-trees have now grown up. I should have liked to erect a cross, but that would not have done, you know—after all, she was not a Christian."

"And what of Pechorin?" I asked.

"Pechorin was ill for a long time, and grew thin, poor fellow; but we never spoke of Bela from that time forth. I saw that it would be disagreeable to him, so what would have been the use? About three months later he was appointed to the E——Regiment, and departed for Georgia. We have never met since. Yet, when I come to think of it, somebody told me not long ago that he had returned to Russia—but it was not in the general orders for the corps. Besides, to the like of us news is late in coming."

Hereupon—probably to drown sad memories—he launched forth into a lengthy dissertation on the unpleasantness of learning news a year late.

I did not interrupt him, nor did I listen.

In an hour's time a chance of proceeding on our journey presented itself. The snowstorm subsided, the sky became clear, and we set off. On the way I involuntarily let the conversation turn on Bela and Pechorin.

"You have not heard what became of Kazbich?" I asked.

"Kazbich? In truth, I don't know. I have heard that with the Shapsugs, on our right flank, there is a certain Kazbich, a dare-devil fellow who rides about at a walking pace, in a red tunic, under our bullets, and bows politely whenever one hums near him—but it can scarcely be the same person!"...

In Kobi, Maksim Maksimych and I parted company. I posted on, and he, on account of his heavy luggage, was unable to follow me. We had no expectation of ever meeting again, but meet we did, and, if you like, I will tell you how—it is quite a history... You must acknowledge, though, that Maksim Maksimych is a man worthy of all respect... If you admit that, I shall be fully rewarded for my, perhaps, too lengthy story.

# BOOK II

# MAKSIM MAKSIMYCH

AFTER parting with Maksim Maksimych, I galloped briskly through the gorges of the Terek and Darial, breakfasted in Kazbek, drank tea in Lars, and arrived at Vladikavkaz in time for supper. I spare you a description of the mountains, as well as exclamations which convey no meaning, and word-paintings which convey no image—especially to those who have never been in the Caucasus. I also omit statistical observations, which I am quite sure nobody would read.

I put up at the inn which is frequented by all who travel in those parts, and where, by the way, there is no one you can order to roast your pheasant and cook your cabbage-soup, because the three veterans who have charge of the inn are either so stupid, or so drunk, that it is impossible to knock any sense at all out of them.

I was informed that I should have to stay there three days longer, because the "Adventure" had not yet arrived from Ekaterinograd and consequently could not start on the return journey. What a misadventure! [19] ... But a bad pun is no consolation to a Russian, and, for the sake of something to occupy my thoughts, I took it into my head to write down the story about Bela, which I had heard from Maksim Maksimych—never imagining that it would be the first link in a long chain of novels: you see how an insignificant event has sometimes dire results!... Perhaps, however, you do not know what the "Adventure" is? It is a convoy—composed of half a company of infantry, with a cannon—which escorts baggage-trains through Kabardia from Vladikavkaz to Ekaterinograd.

The first day I found the time hang on my hands dreadfully. Early next morning a vehicle drove into the courtyard... Aha! Maksim Maksimych!... We met like a couple of old friends. I offered to share my own room with him, and he accepted my hospitality without standing upon ceremony; he even clapped me on the shoulder and puckered up his mouth by way of a smile—a queer fellow, that!...

---

[19] In Russian—okaziya=occasion, adventure, etc.; chto za okaziya=how unfortunate!

39

Maksim Maksimych was profoundly versed in the culinary art. He roasted the pheasant astonishingly well and basted it successfully with cucumber sauce. I was obliged to acknowledge that, but for him, I should have had to remain on a dry-food diet. A bottle of Kakhetian wine helped us to forget the modest number of dishes—of which there was one, all told. Then we lit our pipes, took our chairs, and sat down—I by the window, and he by the stove, in which a fire had been lighted because the day was damp and cold. We remained silent. What had we to talk about? He had already told me all that was of interest about himself and I had nothing to relate. I looked out of the window. Here and there, behind the trees, I caught glimpses of a number of poor, low houses straggling along the bank of the Terek, which flowed seaward in an ever-widening stream; farther off rose the dark-blue, jagged wall of the mountains, behind which Mount Kazbek gazed forth in his high priest's hat of white. I took a mental farewell of them; I felt sorry to leave them...

Thus we sat for a considerable time. The sun was sinking behind the cold summits and a whitish mist was beginning to spread over the valleys, when the silence was broken by the jingling of the bell of a travelling-carriage and the shouting of drivers in the street. A few vehicles, accompanied by dirty Armenians, drove into the courtyard of the inn, and behind them came an empty travelling-carriage. Its light movement, comfortable arrangement, and elegant appearance gave it a kind of foreign stamp. Behind it walked a man with large moustaches. He was wearing a Hungarian jacket and was rather well dressed for a manservant. From the bold manner in which he shook the ashes out of his pipe and shouted at the coachman it was impossible to mistake his calling. He was obviously the spoiled servant of an indolent master—something in the nature of a Russian Figaro.

"Tell me, my good man," I called to him out of the window. "What is it?— Has the 'Adventure' arrived, eh?"

He gave me a rather insolent glance, straightened his cravat, and turned away. An Armenian, who was walking near him, smiled and answered for him that the "Adventure" had, in fact, arrived, and would start on the return journey the following morning.

"Thank heavens!" said Maksim Maksimych, who had come up to the window at that moment. "What a wonderful carriage!" he added; "probably it belongs to some official who is going to Tiflis for a judicial inquiry. You can see that he is unacquainted with our little mountains! No, my friend, you're not serious! They are not for the like of you; why, they would shake even an English carriage to bits!—But who could it be? Let us go and find out."

We went out into the corridor, at the end of which there was an open door leading into a side room. The manservant and a driver were dragging portmanteaux into the room.

"I say, my man!" the staff-captain asked him: "Whose is that marvelous carriage?—Eh?—A beautiful carriage!"

Without turning round the manservant growled something to himself as he undid a portmanteau. Maksim Maksimych grew angry.

"I am speaking to you, my friend!" he said, touching the uncivil fellow on the shoulder.

"Whose carriage?—My master's."

"And who is your master?"

"Pechorin—"

"What did you say? What? Pechorin?—Great Heavens!... Did he not serve in the Caucasus?" exclaimed Maksim Maksimych, plucking me by the sleeve. His eyes were sparkling with joy.

"Yes, he served there, I think—but I have not been with him long."

"Well! Just so!... Just so!... Grigori Aleksandrovich?... that is his name, of course? Your master and I were friends," he added, giving the manservant a friendly clap on the shoulder with such force as to cause him to stagger.

"Excuse me, sir, you are hindering me," said the latter, frowning.

"What a fellow you are, my friend! Why, don't you know, your master and I were bosom friends, and lived together?... But where has he put up?"

The servant intimated that Pechorin had stayed to take supper and pass the night at Colonel N——'s.

"But won't he be looking in here in the evening?" said Maksim Maksimych. "Or, you, my man, won't you be going over to him for something?... If you do, tell him that Maksim Maksimych is here; just say that—he'll know!—I'll give you half a ruble for a tip!"

The manservant made a scornful face on hearing such a modest promise, but he assured Maksim Maksimych that he would execute his commission.

"He'll be sure to come running up directly!" said Maksim Maksimych, with an air of triumph. "I will go outside the gate and wait for him! Ah, it's a pity I am not acquainted with Colonel N——!"

Maksim Maksimych sat down on a little bench outside the gate, and I went to my room. I confess that I also was awaiting this Pechorin's appearance with a certain amount of impatience—although, from the staff-captain's story, I had formed a by no means favorable idea of him. Still, certain traits in his character struck me as remarkable. In an hour's time one of the old soldiers brought a steaming samovar and a teapot.

"Won't you have some tea, Maksim Maksimych?" I called out of the window.

"Thank you. I am not thirsty, somehow."

"Oh, do have some! It is late, you know, and cold!"

"No, thank you"...

"Well, just as you like!"

I began my tea alone. About ten minutes afterwards my old captain came in.

"You are right, you know; it would be better to have a drop of tea—but I was waiting for Pechorin. His man has been gone a long time now, but evidently something has detained him."

The staff-captain hurriedly sipped a cup of tea, refused a second, and went off again outside the gate—not without a certain amount of disquietude. It was obvious that the old man was mortified by Pechorin's neglect, the more so because a short time previously he had been telling me of their friendship, and up to an hour ago had been convinced that Pechorin would come running up immediately on hearing his name.

It was already late and dark when I opened the window again and began to call Maksim Maksimych, saying that it was time to go to bed. He muttered something through his teeth. I repeated my invitation—he made no answer.

I left a candle on the stove-seat, and, wrapping myself up in my cloak, I lay down on the couch and soon fell into slumber; and I would have slept on quietly had not Maksim Maksimych awakened me as he came into the room. It was then very late. He threw his pipe on the table, began to walk up and down the room, and to rattle about at the stove. At last he lay down, but for a long time he kept coughing, spitting, and tossing about.

"The bugs are biting you, are they not?" I asked.

"Yes, that is it," he answered, with a heavy sigh.

I woke early the next morning, but Maksim Maksimych had anticipated me. I found him sitting on the little bench at the gate.

"I have to go to the Commandant," he said, "so, if Pechorin comes, please send for me."...

I gave my promise. He ran off as if his limbs had regained their youthful strength and suppleness.

The morning was fresh and lovely. Golden clouds had massed themselves on the mountaintops like a new range of aerial mountains. Before the gate a wide square spread out; behind it the bazaar was seething with people, the day being Sunday. Barefooted Ossete boys, carrying wallets of honeycomb on their shoulders, were hovering around me. I cursed them; I had other things to think of—I was beginning to share the worthy staff-captain's uneasiness.

Before ten minutes had passed the man we were awaiting appeared at the end of the square. He was walking with Colonel N., who accompanied him as far as the inn, said good-bye to him, and then turned back to the fortress. I immediately despatched one of the old soldiers for Maksim Maksimych.

Pechorin's manservant went out to meet him and informed him that they were going to put to at once; he handed him a box of cigars, received a few orders, and went off about his business. His master lit a cigar, yawned once or twice, and sat down on the bench on the other side of the gate. I must now draw his portrait for you.

He was of medium height. His shapely, slim figure and broad shoulders gave evidence of a strong constitution, capable of enduring all the hardships of a nomad life and changes of climates, and of resisting with success both the demoralizing effects of life in the Capital and the tempests of the soul. His velvet overcoat, which was covered with dust, was fastened by the two lower buttons only, and exposed to view linen of dazzling whiteness, which proved that he had the habits of a gentleman. His gloves, soiled by travel, seemed as though made expressly for his small, aristocratic hand, and when he took one glove off I was astonished at the thinness of his pale fingers. His gait was careless and indolent, but I noticed that he did not swing his arms—a sure sign of a certain secretiveness of character. These remarks, however, are the result of my own observations, and I have not the least desire to make you blindly believe in them. When he was in the act of seating himself on the bench his upright figure bent as if there was not a single bone in his back. The attitude of his whole body was expressive of a certain nervous weakness; he looked, as he sat, like one of Balzac's thirty-year-old coquettes resting in her downy arm-chair after a fatiguing ball. From my first glance at his face

I should not have supposed his age to be more than twenty-three, though afterwards I should have put it down as thirty. His smile had something of a child-like quality. His skin possessed a kind of feminine delicacy. His fair hair, naturally curly, most picturesquely outlined his pale and noble brow, on which it was only after lengthy observation that traces could be noticed of wrinkles, intersecting each other: probably they showed up more distinctly in moments of anger or mental disturbance. Notwithstanding the light color of his hair, his moustaches and eyebrows were black—a sign of breeding in a man, just as a black mane and a black tail in a white horse. To complete the portrait, I will add that he had a slightly turned-up nose, teeth of dazzling whiteness, and brown eyes—I must say a few words more about his eyes.

In the first place, they never laughed when he laughed. Have you not happened, yourself, to notice the same peculiarity in certain people?... It is a sign either of an evil disposition or of deep and constant grief. From behind his half-lowered eyelashes they shone with a kind of phosphorescent gleam—if I may so express myself—which was not the reflection of a fervid soul or of a playful fancy, but a glitter like to that of smooth steel, blinding but cold. His glance—brief, but piercing and heavy— left the unpleasant impression of an indiscreet question and might have seemed insolent had it not been so unconcernedly tranquil.

It may be that all these remarks came into my mind only after I had known some details of his life, and it may be, too, that his appearance would have produced an entirely different impression upon another; but, as you will not hear of him from anyone except myself, you will have to rest content, nolens volens, with the description I have given. In conclusion, I will say that, speaking generally, he was a very good-looking man, and had one of those original types of countenance which are particularly pleasing to women.

The horses were already put to; now and then the bell jingled on the shaft-bow; [20] and the manservant had twice gone up to Pechorin with the announcement that everything was ready, but still there was no sign of Maksim Maksimych. Fortunately Pechorin was sunk in thought as he gazed at the jagged, blue peaks of the Caucasus, and was apparently by no means in a hurry for the road.

I went up to him.

"If you care to wait a little longer," I said, "you will have the pleasure of meeting an old friend."

---

[20] The duga.

44

"Oh, exactly!" he answered quickly. "They told me so yesterday. Where is he, though?"

I looked in the direction of the square and there I descried Maksim Maksimych running as hard as he could. In a few moments he was beside us. He was scarcely able to breathe; perspiration was rolling in large drops from his face; wet tufts of grey hair, escaping from under his cap, were glued to his forehead; his knees were shaking... He was about to throw himself on Pechorin's neck, but the latter, rather coldly, though with a smile of welcome, stretched out his hand to him. For a moment the staffcaptain was petrified, but then eagerly seized Pechorin's hand in both his own. He was still unable to speak.

"How glad I am to see you, my dear Maksim Maksimych! Well, how are you?" said Pechorin.

"And... thou... you?" [21] murmured the old man, with tears in his eyes. "What an age it is since I have seen you!... But where are you off to?"...

"I am going to Persia—and farther."...

"But surely not immediately?... Wait a little, my dear fellow!... Surely we are not going to part at once?... What a long time it is since we have seen each other!"...

"It is time for me to go, Maksim Maksimych," was the reply.

"Good heavens, good heavens! But where are you going to in such a hurry? There was so much I should have liked to tell you! So much to question you about!... Well, what of yourself? Have you retired?... What?... How have you been getting along?"

"Getting bored!" answered Pechorin, smiling.

"You remember the life we led in the fortress? A splendid country for hunting! You were awfully fond of shooting, you know!... And Bela?"...

Pechorin turned just the slightest bit pale and averted his head.

"Yes, I remember!" he said, almost immediately forcing a yawn.

Maksim Maksimych began to beg him to stay with him for a couple of hours or so longer.

---

[21] "Thou" is the form of address used in speaking to an intimate friend, etc. Pechorin had used the more formal "you."

"We will have a splendid dinner," he said. "I have two pheasants; and the Kakhetian wine is excellent here... not what it is in Georgia, of course, but still of the best sort... We will have a talk... You will tell me about your life in Petersburg... Eh?"...

"In truth, there's nothing for me to tell, dear Maksim Maksimych... However, good-bye, it is time for me to be off... I am in a hurry... I thank you for not having forgotten me," he added, taking him by the hand.

The old man knit his brows. He was grieved and angry, although he tried to hide his feelings.

"Forget!" he growled. "I have not forgotten anything... Well, God be with you!... It is not like this that I thought we should meet."

"Come! That will do, that will do!" said Pechorin, giving him a friendly embrace. "Is it possible that I am not the same as I used to be?... What can we do? Everyone must go his own way... Are we ever going to meet again?—God only knows!"

While saying this he had taken his seat in the carriage, and the coachman was already gathering up the reins.

"Wait, wait!" cried Maksim Maksimych suddenly, holding on to the carriage door. "I was nearly forgetting altogether. Your papers were left with me, Grigori Aleksandrovich... I drag them about everywhere I go... I thought I should find you in Georgia, but this is where it has pleased Heaven that we should meet. What's to be done with them?"...

"Whatever you like!" answered Pechorin. "Good-bye."...

"So you are off to Persia?... But when will you return?" Maksim Maksimych cried after him.

By this time the carriage was a long way off, but Pechorin made a sign with his hand which might be interpreted as meaning:

"It is doubtful whether I shall return, and there is no reason, either, why I should!"

The jingle of the bell and the clatter of the wheels along the flinty road had long ceased to be audible, but the poor old man still remained standing in the same place, deep in thought.

"Yes," he said at length, endeavoring to assume an air of indifference, although from time to time a tear of vexation glistened on his eyelashes. "Of course we were friends—well, but what are friends nowadays?... What

46

could I be to him? I'm not rich; I've no rank; and, moreover, I'm not at all his match in years!—See what a dandy he has become since he has been staying in Petersburg again!... What a carriage!... What a quantity of luggage!... And such a haughty manservant too!"...

These words were pronounced with an ironical smile.

"Tell me," he continued, turning to me, "what do you think of it? Come, what the devil is he off to Persia for now?... Good Lord, it is ridiculous—ridiculous!... But I always knew that he was a fickle man, and one you could never rely on!... But, indeed, it is a pity that he should come to a bad end... yet it can't be otherwise!... I always did say that there is no good to be got out of a man who forgets his old friends!"...

Hereupon he turned away in order to hide his agitation and proceeded to walk about the courtyard, around his cart, pretending to be examining the wheels, whilst his eyes kept filling with tears every moment.

"Maksim Maksimych," I said, going up to him, "what papers are these that Pechorin left you?"

"Goodness knows! Notes of some sort"...

"What will you do with them?"

"What? I'll have cartridges made of them."

"Hand them over to me instead."

He looked at me in surprise, growled something through his teeth, and began to rummage in his portmanteau. Out he drew a writing-book and threw it contemptuously on the ground; then a second—a third—a tenth shared the same fate. There was something childish in his vexation, and it struck me as ridiculous and pitiable...

"Here they are," he said. "I congratulate you on your find!"...

"And I may do anything I like with them?"

"Yes, print them in the newspapers, if you like. What is it to me? Am I a friend or relation of his? It is true that for a long time we lived under one roof... but aren't there plenty of people with whom I have lived?"...

I seized the papers and lost no time in carrying them away, fearing that the staff-captain might repent his action. Soon somebody came to tell us that the "Adventure" would set off in an hour's time. I ordered the horses to be put to.

I had already put my cap on when the staff-captain entered the room. Apparently he had not got ready for departure. His manner was somewhat cold and constrained.

"You are not going, then, Maksim Maksimych?"

"No, sir!"

"But why not?"

"Well, I have not seen the Commandant yet, and I have to deliver some Government things."

"But you did go, you know."

"I did, of course," he stammered, "but he was not at home... and I did not wait."

I understood. For the first time in his life, probably, the poor old man had, to speak by the book, thrown aside official business 'for the sake of his personal requirements'... and how he had been rewarded!

"I am very sorry, Maksim Maksimych, very sorry indeed," I said, "that we must part sooner than necessary."

"What should we rough old men be thinking of to run after you? You young men are fashionable and proud: under the Circassian bullets you are friendly enough with us... but when you meet us afterwards you are ashamed even to give us your hand!"

"I have not deserved these reproaches, Maksim Maksimych."

"Well, but you know I'm quite right. However, I wish you all good luck and a pleasant journey."

We took a rather cold farewell of each other. The kind-hearted Maksim Maksimych had become the obstinate, cantankerous staff-captain! And why? Because Pechorin, through absent-mindedness or from some other cause, had extended his hand to him when Maksim Maksimych was going to throw himself on his neck! Sad it is to see when a young man loses his best hopes and dreams, when from before his eyes is withdrawn the rose-hued veil through which he has looked upon the deeds and feelings of mankind; although there is the hope that the old illusions will be replaced by new ones, none the less evanescent, but, on the other hand, none the less sweet. But wherewith can they be replaced when one is at the age of Maksim Maksimych? Do what you will, the heart hardens and the soul shrinks in upon itself.
I departed—alone.

# FOREWORD TO BOOKS III, IV, AND V
# CONCERNING PECHORIN'S DIARY

I LEARNED not long ago that Pechorin had died on his way back from Persia. The news afforded me great delight; it gave me the right to print these notes; and I have taken advantage of the opportunity of putting my name at the head of another person's productions. Heaven grant that my readers may not punish me for such an innocent deception!

I must now give some explanation of the reasons which have induced me to betray to the public the inmost secrets of a man whom I never knew. If I had even been his friend, well and good: the artful indiscretion of the true friend is intelligible to everybody; but I only saw Pechorin once in my life—on the high-road—and, consequently, I cannot cherish towards him that inexplicable hatred, which, hiding its face under the mask of friendship, awaits but the death or misfortune of the beloved object to burst over its head in a storm of reproaches, admonitions, scoffs and regrets.

On reading over these notes, I have become convinced of the sincerity of the man who has so unsparingly exposed to view his own weaknesses and vices. The history of a man's soul, even the pettiest soul, is hardly less interesting and useful than the history of a whole people; especially when the former is the result of the observations of a mature mind upon itself, and has been written without any egoistical desire of arousing sympathy or astonishment. Rousseau's Confessions has precisely this defect—he read it to his friends.

And, so, it is nothing but the desire to be useful that has constrained me to print fragments of this diary which fell into my hands by chance. Although I have altered all the proper names, those who are mentioned in it will probably recognize themselves, and, it may be, will find some justification for actions for which they have hitherto blamed a man who has ceased henceforth to have anything in common with this world. We almost always excuse that which we understand.

I have inserted in this book only those portions of the diary which refer to Pechorin's sojourn in the Caucasus. There still remains in my hands a thick writing-book in which he tells the story of his whole life. Some time or other that, too, will present itself before the tribunal of the world, but, for many and weighty reasons, I do not venture to take such a responsibility upon myself now.

Possibly some readers would like to know my own opinion of Pechorin's character. My answer is: the title of this book. "But that is malicious irony!" they will say... I know not.

# BOOK III

# THE FIRST EXTRACT FROM PECHORIN'S DIARY

**TAMAN**

TAMAN is the nastiest little hole of all the seaports of Russia. I was all but starved there, to say nothing of having a narrow escape of being drowned.

I arrived late at night by the post-car. The driver stopped the tired troika [22] at the gate of the only stone-built house that stood at the entrance to the town. The sentry, a Cossack from the Black Sea, hearing the jingle of the bell, cried out, sleepily, in his barbarous voice, "Who goes there?" An under-officer of Cossacks and a headborough [23] came out. I explained that I was an officer bound for the active-service detachment on Government business, and I proceeded to demand official quarters. The headborough conducted us round the town. Whatever hut we drove up to we found to be occupied. The weather was cold; I had not slept for three nights; I was tired out, and I began to lose my temper.

"Take me somewhere or other, you scoundrel!" I cried; "to the devil himself, so long as there's a place to put up at!"

"There is one other lodging," answered the headborough, scratching his head. "Only you won't like it, sir. It is uncanny!"

Failing to grasp the exact signification of the last phrase, I ordered him to go on, and, after a lengthy peregrination through muddy byways, at the sides of which I could see nothing but old fences, we drove up to a small cabin, right on the shore of the sea.

The full moon was shining on the little reed-thatched roof and the white walls of my new dwelling. In the courtyard, which was surrounded by a wall of rubble-stone, there stood another miserable hovel, smaller and older than the first and all askew. The shore descended precipitously to the

---

[22] Team of three horses abreast.

[23] Desyatnik, a superintendent of ten (men or huts), i.e. an officer like the old English tithing-man or headborough.

sea, almost from its very walls, and down below, with incessant murmur, plashed the dark-blue waves. The moon gazed softly upon the watery element, restless but obedient to it, and I was able by its light to distinguish two ships lying at some distance from the shore, their black rigging motionless and standing out, like cobwebs, against the pale line of the horizon.

"There are vessels in the harbor," I said to myself. "To-morrow I will set out for Gelenjik."

I had with me, in the capacity of soldier-servant, a Cossack of the frontier army. Ordering him to take down the portmanteau and dismiss the driver, I began to call the master of the house. No answer! I knocked—all was silent within!... What could it mean? At length a boy of about fourteen crept out from the hall.

"Where is the master?"

"There isn't one."

"What! No master?"

"None!"

"And the mistress?"

"She has gone off to the village."

"Who will open the door for me, then?" I said, giving it a kick.

The door opened of its own accord, and a breath of moisture-laden air was wafted from the hut. I struck a lucifer match and held it to the boy's face. It lit up two white eyes. He was totally blind, obviously so from birth. He stood stock-still before me, and I began to examine his features.

I confess that I have a violent prejudice against all blind, one-eyed, deaf, dumb, legless, armless, hunchbacked, and such-like people. I have observed that there is always a certain strange connection between a man's exterior and his soul; as, if when the body loses a limb, the soul also loses some power of feeling.

And so I began to examine the blind boy's face. But what could be read upon a face from which the eyes are missing?... For a long time I gazed at him with involuntary compassion, when suddenly a scarcely perceptible smile flitted over his thin lips, producing, I know not why, a most unpleasant impression upon me. I began to feel a suspicion that the blind boy was not so blind as he appeared to be. In vain I endeavored to convince myself that it was impossible to counterfeit cataracts; and besides, what reason could there be for doing such a thing? But I could not help my suspicions. I am easily swayed by prejudice...

"You are the master's son?" I asked at length.

"No."

"Who are you, then?"

"An orphan—a poor boy."

"Has the mistress any children?"

"No, her daughter ran away and crossed the sea with a Tartar."

"What sort of a Tartar?"

"The devil only knows! A Crimean Tartar, a boatman from Kerch."

I entered the hut. Its whole furniture consisted of two benches and a table, together with an enormous chest beside the stove. There was not a single icon to be seen on the wall—a bad sign! The sea-wind burst in through the broken window-pane. I drew a wax candle-end from my portmanteau, lit it, and began to put my things out. My sabre and gun I placed in a corner, my pistols I laid on the table. I spread my felt cloak out on one bench, and the Cossack his on the other. In ten minutes the latter was snoring, but I could not go to sleep—the image of the boy with the white eyes kept hovering before me in the dark.

About an hour passed thus. The moon shone in at the window and its rays played along the earthen floor of the hut. Suddenly a shadow flitted across the bright strip of moonshine which intersected the floor. I raised myself up a little and glanced out of the window. Again somebody ran by it and disappeared—goodness knows where! It seemed impossible for anyone to descend the steep cliff overhanging the shore, but that was the only thing that could have happened. I rose, threw on my tunic, girded on a dagger, and with the utmost quietness went out of the hut. The blind boy was coming towards me. I hid by the fence, and he passed by me with a sure but cautious step. He was carrying a parcel under his arm. He turned towards the harbor and began to descend a steep and narrow path.

"On that day the dumb will cry out and the blind will see," I said to myself, following him just close enough to keep him in sight.

Meanwhile the moon was becoming overcast by clouds and a mist had risen upon the sea. The lantern alight in the stern of a ship close at hand was scarcely visible through the mist, and by the shore there glimmered the foam of the waves, which every moment threatened to submerge it. Descending with difficulty, I stole along the steep declivity, and all at once I saw the blind boy come to a standstill and then turn down to the right. He walked so close to the water's edge that it seemed as if the waves would straightway seize him and carry him off. But, judging by the confidence with which he stepped from rock to rock and avoided the water-channels, this was evidently not the first time that he had made that journey. Finally he stopped, as though listening for something, squatted down upon the ground, and laid the parcel beside him. Concealing myself behind a projecting rock on the shore, I kept watch on his movements. After a few minutes a white figure made its appearance from the opposite direction. It came up to the blind boy and sat down beside him. At times the wind wafted their conversation to me.

"Well?" said a woman's voice. "The storm is violent; Yanko will not be here."

"Yanko is not afraid of the storm!" the other replied.

"The mist is thickening," rejoined the woman's voice, sadness in its tone.

"In the mist it is all the easier to slip past the guardships," was the answer.

"And if he is drowned?"

"Well, what then? On Sunday you won't have a new ribbon to go to church in."

An interval of silence followed. One thing, however, struck me—in talking to me the blind boy spoke in the Little Russian dialect, but now he was expressing himself in pure Russian.

"You see, I am right!" the blind boy went on, clapping his hands. "Yanko is not afraid of sea, nor winds, nor mist, nor coastguards! Just listen! That is not the water plashing, you can't deceive me—it is his long oars."

The woman sprang up and began anxiously to gaze into the distance.

"You are raving!" she said. "I cannot see anything."

I confess that, much as I tried to make out in the distance something resembling a boat, my efforts were unsuccessful. About ten minutes passed thus, when a black speck appeared between the mountains of the waves! At one time it grew larger, at another smaller. Slowly rising upon the crests of the waves and swiftly descending from them, the boat drew near to the shore.

53

"He must be a brave sailor," I thought, "to have determined to cross the twenty versts of strait on a night like this, and he must have had a weighty reason for doing so."

Reflecting thus, I gazed with an involuntary beating of the heart at the poor boat. It dived like a duck, and then, with rapidly swinging oars—like wings—it sprang forth from the abyss amid the splashes of the foam. "Ah!" I thought, "it will be dashed against the shore with all its force and broken to pieces!" But it turned aside adroitly and leaped unharmed into a little creek. Out of it stepped a man of medium height, wearing a Tartar sheepskin cap. He waved his hand, and all three set to work to drag something out of the boat. The cargo was so large that, to this day, I cannot understand how it was that the boat did not sink.

Each of them shouldered a bundle, and they set off along the shore, and I soon lost sight of them. I had to return home; but I confess I was rendered uneasy by all these strange happenings, and I found it hard to await the morning.

My Cossack was very much astonished when, on waking up, he saw me fully dressed. I did not, however, tell him the reason. For some time I stood at the window, gazing admiringly at the blue sky all studded with wisps of cloud, and at the distant shore of the Crimea, stretching out in a lilac-colored streak and ending in a cliff, on the summit of which the white tower of the lighthouse was gleaming. Then I betook myself to the fortress, Phanagoriya, in order to ascertain from the Commandant at what hour I should depart for Gelenjik.

But the Commandant, alas! could not give me any definite information. The vessels lying in the harbor were all either guard-ships or merchant-vessels which had not yet even begun to take in lading.

"Maybe in about three or four days' time a mail-boat will come in," said the Commandant, "and then we shall see."

I returned home sulky and wrathful. My Cossack met me at the door with a frightened countenance.

"Things are looking bad, sir!" he said.

"Yes, my friend; goodness only knows when we shall get away!"

Hereupon he became still more uneasy, and, bending towards me, he said in a whisper:

"It is uncanny here! I met an under-officer from the Black Sea to-day—he's an acquaintance of mine—he was in my detachment last year. When I told him where we were staying, he said, 'That place is uncanny, old fellow; they're wicked people there!'... And, indeed, what sort of a blind boy is that? He goes everywhere alone, to fetch water and to buy bread at the bazaar. It is evident they have become accustomed to that sort of thing here."

"Well, what then? Tell me, though, has the mistress of the place put in an appearance?"

"During your absence to-day, an old woman and her daughter arrived."

"What daughter? She has no daughter!"

"Goodness knows who it can be if it isn't her daughter; but the old woman is sitting over there in the hut now."

I entered the hovel. A blazing fire was burning in the stove, and they were cooking a dinner which struck me as being a rather luxurious one for poor people. To all my questions the old woman replied that she was deaf and could not hear me. There was nothing to be got out of her. I turned to the blind boy who was sitting in front of the stove, putting twigs into the fire.

"Now, then, you little blind devil," I said, taking him by the ear. "Tell me, where were you roaming with the bundle last night, eh?"

The blind boy suddenly burst out weeping, shrieking and wailing.

"Where did I go? I did not go anywhere... With the bundle?... What bundle?"

This time the old woman heard, and she began to mutter:

"Hark at them plotting, and against a poor boy too! What are you touching him for? What has he done to you?"

I had enough of it, and went out, firmly resolved to find the key to the riddle.

I wrapped myself up in my felt cloak and, sitting down on a rock by the fence, gazed into the distance. Before me stretched the sea, agitated by the storm of the previous night, and its monotonous roar, like the murmur of a town over which slumber is beginning to creep, recalled bygone years to my mind, and transported my thoughts northward to our cold Capital. Agitated by my recollections, I became oblivious of my surroundings.

About an hour passed thus, perhaps even longer. Suddenly something resembling a song struck upon my ear. It was a song, and the voice was a woman's, young and fresh—but, where was it coming from?... I listened; it was a harmonious melody—now long-drawnout and plaintive, now swift and lively. I looked around me—there was nobody to be seen. I listened again—the sounds seemed to be falling from the sky. I raised my eyes. On the roof of my cabin was standing a young girl in a striped dress and with her hair hanging loose—a regular water-nymph. Shading her eyes from the sun's rays with the palm of her hand, she was gazing intently into the distance. At one time, she would laugh and talk to herself, at another, she would strike up her song anew.

I have retained that song in my memory, word for word:

> At their own free will
> They seem to wander
> O'er the green sea yonder,
> Those ships, as still
> They are onward going,
> With white sails flowing.
> And among those ships
> My eye can mark
> My own dear barque:
> By two oars guided
> (All unprovided
> With sails) it slips.
> The storm-wind raves:
> And the old ships—see!
> With wings spread free,
> Over the waves
> They scatter and flee!
> The sea I will hail
> With obeisance deep:
> "Thou base one, hark!
> Thou must not fail
> My little barque
> From harm to keep!"
> For lo! 'tis bearing
> Most precious gear,
> And brave and daring
> The arms that steer
> Within the dark
> My little barque.

Involuntarily the thought occurred to me that I had heard the same voice the night before. I reflected for a moment, and when I looked up at the roof again there was no girl to be seen. Suddenly she darted past me, with another song on her lips, and, snapping her fingers, she ran up to the old woman. Thereupon a quarrel arose between them. The old woman grew angry, and the girl laughed loudly. And then I saw my Undine running and gambolling again. She came up to where I was, stopped, and gazed fixedly into my face as if surprised at my presence. Then she turned carelessly away and went quietly towards the harbor. But this was not all. The whole day she kept hovering around my lodging, singing and gambolling without a moment's interruption. Strange creature! There was not the slightest sign of insanity in her face; on the contrary, her eyes, which were continually resting upon me, were bright and piercing. Moreover, they seemed to be endowed with a certain magnetic power, and each time they looked at me they appeared to be expecting a question. But I had only to open my lips to speak, and away she would run, with a sly smile.

Certainly never before had I seen a woman like her. She was by no means beautiful; but, as in other matters, I have my own prepossessions on the subject of beauty. There was a good deal of breeding in her... Breeding in women, as in horses, is a great thing: a discovery, the credit of which belongs to young France. It—that is to say, breeding, not young France—is chiefly to be detected in the gait, in the hands and feet; the nose, in particular, is of the greatest significance. In Russia a straight nose is rarer than a small foot.

My songstress appeared to be not more than eighteen years of age. The unusual suppleness of her figure, the characteristic and original way she had of inclining her head, her long, light-brown hair, the golden sheen of her slightly sunburnt neck and shoulders, and especially her straight nose—all these held me fascinated. Although in her sidelong glances I could read a certain wildness and disdain, although in her smile there was a certain vagueness, yet—such is the force of predilections—that straight nose of hers drove me crazy. I fancied that I had found Goethe's Mignon— that queer creature of his German imagination. And, indeed, there was a good deal of similarity between them; the same rapid transitions from the utmost restlessness to complete immobility, the same enigmatical speeches, the same gambols, the same strange songs.

Towards evening I stopped her at the door and entered into the following conversation with her.

"Tell me, my beauty," I asked, "what were you doing on the roof to-day?"

"I was looking to see from what direction the wind was blowing."

"What did you want to know for?"

"Whence the wind blows comes happiness."

"Well? Were you invoking happiness with your song?"

"Where there is singing there is also happiness."

"But what if your song were to bring you sorrow?"

"Well, what then? Where things won't be better, they will be worse; and from bad to good again is not far."

"And who taught you that song?"

"Nobody taught me; it comes into my head and I sing; whoever is to hear it, he will hear it, and whoever ought not to hear it, he will not understand it."

"What is your name, my songstress?"

"He who baptized me knows."

"And who baptized you?"

"How should I know?"

"What a secretive girl you are! But look here, I have learned something about you"—she neither changed countenance nor moved her lips, as though my discovery was of no concern to her—"I have learned that you went to the shore last night."

And, thereupon, I very gravely retailed to her all that I had seen, thinking that I should embarrass her. Not a bit of it! She burst out laughing heartily.

"You have seen much, but know little; and what you do know, see that you keep it under lock and key."

"But supposing, now, I was to take it into my head to inform the Commandant?" and here I assumed a very serious, not to say stern, demeanour.

She gave a sudden spring, began to sing, and hid herself like a bird frightened out of a thicket. My last words were altogether out of place. I had no suspicion then how momentous they were, but afterwards I had occasion to rue them.

As soon as the dusk of evening fell, I ordered the Cossack to heat the teapot, campaign fashion. I lighted a candle and sat down by the table, smoking my travelling-pipe. I was just about to finish my second tumbler of tea when suddenly the door creaked and I heard behind me the sound of footsteps and the light rustle of a dress. I started and turned round.

58

It was she—my Undine. Softly and without saying a word she sat down opposite to me and fixed her eyes upon me. Her glance seemed wondrously tender, I know not why; it reminded me of one of those glances which, in years gone by, so despotically played with my life. She seemed to be waiting for a question, but I kept silence, filled with an inexplicable sense of embarrassment. Mental agitation was evinced by the dull pallor which overspread her countenance; her hand, which I noticed was trembling slightly, moved aimlessly about the table. At one time her breast heaved, and at another she seemed to be holding her breath. This little comedy was beginning to pall upon me, and I was about to break the silence in a most prosaic manner, that is, by offering her a glass of tea; when suddenly, springing up, she threw her arms around my neck, and I felt her moist, fiery lips pressed upon mine. Darkness came before my eyes, my head began to swim. I embraced her with the whole strength of youthful passion. But, like a snake, she glided from between my arms, whispering in my ear as she did so:

"To-night, when everyone is asleep, go out to the shore."

Like an arrow she sprang from the room.

In the hall she upset the teapot and a candle which was standing on the floor.

"Little devil!" cried the Cossack, who had taken up his position on the straw and had contemplated warming himself with the remains of the tea.

It was only then that I recovered my senses.

In about two hours' time, when all had grown silent in the harbor, I awakened my Cossack.

"If I fire a pistol," I said, "run to the shore."

He stared open-eyed and answered mechanically:

"Very well, sir."

I stuffed a pistol in my belt and went out. She was waiting for me at the edge of the cliff. Her attire was more than light, and a small kerchief girded her supple waist.

"Follow me!" she said, taking me by the hand, and we began to descend.

I cannot understand how it was that I did not break my neck. Down below we turned to the right and proceeded to take the path along which I had followed the blind boy the evening before. The moon had not yet risen, and only two little stars, like two guardian lighthouses, were twinkling in the dark-blue vault of heaven. The heavy waves, with measured and even motion, rolled one after the other, scarcely lifting the solitary boat which was moored to the shore.

"Let us get into the boat," said my companion.

I hesitated. I am no lover of sentimental trips on the sea; but this was not the time to draw back. She leaped into the boat, and I after her; and I had not time to recover my wits before I observed that we were adrift.

"What is the meaning of this?" I said angrily.

"It means," she answered, seating me on the bench and throwing her arms around my waist, "it means that I love you!"...

Her cheek was pressed close to mine, and I felt her burning breath upon my face. Suddenly something fell noisily into the water. I clutched at my belt—my pistol was gone! Ah, now a terrible suspicion crept into my soul, and the blood rushed to my head! I looked round. We were about fifty fathoms from the shore, and I could not swim a stroke! I tried to thrust her away from me, but she clung like a cat to my clothes, and suddenly a violent wrench all but threw me into the sea. The boat rocked, but I righted myself, and a desperate struggle began.

Fury lent me strength, but I soon found that I was no match for my opponent in point of agility...

"What do you want?" I cried, firmly squeezing her little hands.

Her fingers crunched, but her serpent-like nature bore up against the torture, and she did not utter a cry.

"You saw us," she answered. "You will tell on us."

And, with a supernatural effort, she flung me on to the side of the boat; we both hung half overboard; her hair touched the water. The decisive moment had come. I planted my knee against the bottom of the boat, caught her by the tresses with one hand and by the throat with the other; she let go my clothes, and, in an instant, I had thrown her into the waves.

It was now rather dark; once or twice her head appeared for an instant amidst the sea foam, and I saw no more of her.

I found the half of an old oar at the bottom of the boat, and somehow or other, after lengthy efforts, I made fast to the harbor. Making my way along the shore towards my hut, I involuntarily gazed in the direction of the spot where, on the previous night, the blind boy had awaited the nocturnal mariner. The moon was already rolling through the sky, and it seemed to me that somebody in white was sitting on the shore. Spurred by curiosity, I crept up and crouched down in the grass on the top of the cliff. By thrusting my head out a little way I was able to get a good view of everything that was happening down below, and I was not very much astonished, but almost rejoiced, when I recognized my water-nymph. She was wringing the seafoam from her long hair. Her wet garment outlined her supple figure and her high bosom.

Soon a boat appeared in the distance; it drew near rapidly; and, as on the night before, a man in a Tartar cap stepped out of it, but he now had his hair cropped round in the Cossack fashion, and a large knife was sticking out behind his leather belt.

"Yanko," the girl said, "all is lost!"

Then their conversation continued, but so softly that I could not catch a word of it.

"But where is the blind boy?" said Yanko at last, raising his voice.

"I have told him to come," was the reply.

After a few minutes the blind boy appeared, dragging on his back a sack, which they placed in the boat.

"Listen!" said Yanko to the blind boy. "Guard that place! You know where I mean? There are valuable goods there. Tell"—I could not catch the name—"that I am no longer his servant. Things have gone badly. He will see me no more. It is dangerous now. I will go seek work in another place, and he will never be able to find another dare-devil like me. Tell him also that if he had paid me a little better for my labors, I would not have forsaken him. For me there is a way anywhere, if only the wind blows and the sea roars."

After a short silence Yanko continued.

"She is coming with me. It is impossible for her to remain here. Tell the old woman that it is time for her to die; she has been here a long time, and the line must be drawn somewhere. As for us, she will never see us anymore."

"And I?" said the blind boy in a plaintive voice.

"What use have I for you?" was the answer.

In the meantime my Undine had sprung into the boat. She beckoned to her companion with her hand. He placed something in the blind boy's hand and added:

"There, buy yourself some gingerbreads."

"Is this all?" said the blind boy.

"Well, here is some more."

The money fell and jingled as it struck the rock.

The blind boy did not pick it up. Yanko took his seat in the boat; the wind was blowing from the shore; they hoisted the little sail and sped rapidly away. For a long time the white sail gleamed in the moonlight amid the dark waves. Still the blind boy remained seated upon the shore, and then I heard something which sounded like sobbing. The blind boy was, in fact, weeping, and for a long, long time his tears flowed... I grew heavy-hearted. For what reason should fate have thrown me into the peaceful circle of honorable smugglers? Like a stone cast into a smooth well, I had disturbed their quietude, and I barely escaped going to the bottom like a stone.

I returned home. In the hall the burnt-out candle was spluttering on a wooden platter, and my Cossack, contrary to orders, was fast asleep, with his gun held in both hands. I left him at rest, took the candle, and entered the hut. Alas! my cashbox, my sabre with the silver chasing, my Daghestan dagger—the gift of a friend—all had vanished! It was then that I guessed what articles the cursed blind boy had been dragging along. Roughly shaking the Cossack, I woke him up, rated him, and lost my temper. But what was the good of that? And would it not have been ridiculous to complain to the authorities that I had been robbed by a blind boy and all but drowned by an eighteen-year-old girl?

Thank heaven an opportunity of getting away presented itself in the morning, and I left Taman.

What became of the old woman and the poor blind boy I know not. And, besides, what are the joys and sorrows of mankind to me—me, a travelling officer, and one, moreover, with an order for post-horses on Government business?

# BOOK IV

# THE SECOND EXTRACT FROM PECHORIN'S DIARY

## THE FATALIST

I ONCE happened to spend a couple of weeks in a Cossack village on our left flank. A battalion of infantry was stationed there; and it was the custom of the officers to meet at each other's quarters in turn and play cards in the evening.

On one occasion—it was at Major S——'s—finding our game of Boston not sufficiently absorbing, we threw the cards under the table and sat on for a long time, talking. The conversation, for once in a way, was interesting. The subject was the Mussulman tradition that a man's fate is written in heaven, and we discussed the fact that it was gaining many votaries, even amongst our own countrymen. Each of us related various extraordinary occurrences, pro or contra.

"What you have been saying, gentlemen, proves nothing," said the old major. "I presume there is not one of you who has actually been a witness of the strange events which you are citing in support of your opinions?"

"Not one, of course," said many of the guests. "But we have heard of them from trustworthy people."...

"It is all nonsense!" someone said. "Where are the trustworthy people who have seen the Register in which the appointed hour of our death is recorded?... And if predestination really exists, why are free will and reason granted us? Why are we obliged to render an account of our actions?"

At that moment an officer who was sitting in a corner of the room stood up, and, coming slowly to the table, surveyed us all with a quiet and solemn glance. He was a native of Servia, as was evident from his name.

The outward appearance of Lieutenant Vulich was quite in keeping with his character. His height, swarthy complexion, black hair, piercing black eyes, large but straight nose—an attribute of his nation—and the cold and melancholy smile which ever hovered around his lips, all seemed to concur in lending him the appearance of a man apart, incapable of reciprocating the thoughts and passions of those whom fate gave him for companions.

He was brave; talked little, but sharply; confided his thoughts and family secrets to no one; drank hardly a drop of wine; and never dangled after the young Cossack girls, whose charm it is difficult to realize without having seen them. It was said, however, that the colonel's wife was not indifferent to those expressive eyes of his; but he was seriously angry if any hint on the subject was made.

There was only one passion which he did not conceal—the passion for gambling. At the green table he would become oblivious of everything. He usually lost, but his constant ill success only aroused his obstinacy. It was related that, on one occasion, during a nocturnal expedition, he was keeping the bank on a pillow, and had a terrific run of luck. Suddenly shots rang out. The alarm was sounded; all but Vulich jumped up and rushed to arms.

"Stake, va banque!" he cried to one of the most ardent gamblers.

"Seven," the latter answered as he hurried off.

Notwithstanding the general confusion, Vulich calmly finished the deal—seven was the card. By the time he reached the cordon a violent fusillade was in progress. Vulich did not trouble himself about the bullets or the sabres of the Chechenes, but sought for the lucky gambler.

"Seven it was!" he cried out, as at length he perceived him in the cordon of skirmishers who were beginning to dislodge the enemy from the wood; and going up to him, he drew out his purse and pocket-book and handed them to the winner, notwithstanding the latter's objections on the score of the inconvenience of the payment. That unpleasant duty discharged, Vulich dashed forward, carried the soldiers along after him, and, to the very end of the affair, fought the Chechenes with the utmost coolness.

When Lieutenant Vulich came up to the table, we all became silent, expecting to hear, as usual, something original.

"Gentlemen!" he said—and his voice was quiet though lower in tone than usual—"gentlemen, what is the good of futile discussions? You wish for proofs? I propose that we try the experiment on ourselves: whether a man can of his own accord dispose of his life, or whether the fateful moment is appointed beforehand for each of us. Who is agreeable?"

"Not I. Not I," came from all sides.

"There's a queer fellow for you! He does get strange ideas into his head!"

"I propose a wager," I said in jest.

"What sort of wager?"

"I maintain that there is no such thing as predestination," I said, scattering on the table a score or so of ducats—all I had in my pocket.

"Done," answered Vulich in a hollow voice. "Major, you will be judge. Here are fifteen ducats, the remaining five you owe me, kindly add them to the others."

"Very well," said the major; "though, indeed, I do not understand what is the question at issue and how you will decide it!"

Without a word Vulich went into the major's bedroom, and we followed him. He went up to the wall on which the major's weapons were hanging, and took down at random one of the pistols—of which there were several of different calibres. We were still in the dark as to what he meant to do. But, when he cocked the pistol and sprinkled powder in the pan, several of the officers, crying out in spite of themselves, seized him by the arms.

"What are you going to do?" they exclaimed. "This is madness!"

"Gentlemen!" he said slowly, disengaging his arm. "Who would like to pay twenty ducats for me?"

They were silent and drew away.

Vulich went into the other room and sat by the table; we all followed him. With a sign he invited us to sit round him. We obeyed in silence—at that moment he had acquired a certain mysterious authority over us. I stared fixedly into his face; but he met my scrutinising gaze with a quiet and steady glance, and his pallid lips smiled. But, notwithstanding his composure, it seemed to me that I could read the stamp of death upon his pale countenance. I have noticed—and many old soldiers have corroborated my observation—that a man who is to die in a few hours frequently bears on his face a certain strange stamp of inevitable fate, so that it is difficult for practiced eyes to be mistaken.

"You will die to-day!" I said to Vulich.

He turned towards me rapidly, but answered slowly and quietly:

"May be so, maybe not."...

Then, addressing himself to the major, he asked:

"Is the pistol loaded?"

The major, in the confusion, could not quite remember.

"There, that will do, Vulich!" exclaimed somebody. "Of course it must be loaded, if it was one of those hanging on the wall there over our heads. What a man you are for joking!"

"A silly joke, too!" struck in another.

"I wager fifty rubles to five that the pistol is not loaded!" cried a third.

A new bet was made.

I was beginning to get tired of it all.

"Listen," I said, "either shoot yourself, or hang up the pistol in its place and let us go to bed."

"Yes, of course!" many exclaimed. "Let us go to bed."

"Gentlemen, I beg of you not to move," said Vulich, putting the muzzle of the pistol to his forehead.

We were all petrified.

"Mr. Pechorin," he added, "take a card and throw it up in the air."

I took, as I remember now, an ace of hearts off the table and threw it into the air. All held their breath. With eyes full of terror and a certain vague curiosity they glanced rapidly from the pistol to the fateful ace, which slowly descended, quivering in the air. At the moment it touched the table Vulich pulled the trigger... a flash in the pan!

"Thank God!" many exclaimed. "It wasn't loaded!"

"Let us see, though," said Vulich.

He cocked the pistol again, and took aim at a forage-cap which was hanging above the window. A shot rang out. Smoke filled the room; when it cleared away, the forage-cap was taken down. It had been shot right through the center, and the bullet was deeply embedded in the wall.

For two or three minutes no one was able to utter a word. Very quietly Vulich poured my ducats from the major's purse into his own.

Discussions arose as to why the pistol had not gone off the first time. Some maintained that probably the pan had been obstructed; others whispered that the powder had been damp the first time, and that, afterwards, Vulich had sprinkled some fresh powder on it; but I maintained that the last supposition was wrong, because I had not once taken my eyes off the pistol.

"You are lucky at play!" I said to Vulich...

"For the first time in my life!" he answered, with a complacent smile. "It is better than 'bank' and 'shtoss.'" [24]

"But, on the other hand, slightly more dangerous!"

"Well? Have you begun to believe in predestination?

"I do believe in it; only I cannot understand now why it appeared to me that you must inevitably die to-day!"

And this same man, who, such a short time before, had with the greatest calmness aimed a pistol at his own forehead, now suddenly fired up and became embarrassed.

"That will do, though!" he said, rising to his feet. "Our wager is finished, and now your observations, it seems to me, are out of place."

He took up his cap and departed. The whole affair struck me as being strange—and not without reason. Shortly after that, all the officers broke up and went home, discussing Vulich's freaks from different points of view, and, doubtless, with one voice calling me an egoist for having taken up a wager against a man who wanted to shoot himself, as if he could not have found a convenient opportunity without my intervention.

I returned home by the deserted byways of the village. The moon, full and red like the glow of a conflagration, was beginning to make its appearance from behind the jagged horizon of the house-tops; the stars were shining tranquilly in the deep, blue vault of the sky; and I was struck by the absurdity of the idea when I recalled to mind that once upon a time there

---

[24] Card-games.

were some exceedingly wise people who thought that the stars of heaven participated in our insignificant squabbles for a slice of ground, or some other imaginary rights. And what then? These lamps, lighted, so they fancied, only to illuminate their battles and triumphs, are burning with all their former brilliance, whilst the wiseacres themselves, together with their hopes and passions, have long been extinguished, like a little fire kindled at the edge of a forest by a careless wayfarer! But, on the other hand, what strength of will was lent them by the conviction that the entire heavens, with their innumerable habitants, were looking at them with a sympathy, unalterable, though mute!... And we, their miserable descendants, roaming over the earth, without faith, without pride, without enjoyment, and without terror—except that involuntary awe which makes the heart shrink at the thought of the inevitable end—we are no longer capable of great sacrifices, either for the good of mankind or even for our own happiness, because we know the impossibility of such happiness; and, just as our ancestors used to fling themselves from one delusion to another, we pass indifferently from doubt to doubt, without possessing, as they did, either hope or even that vague though, at the same time, keen enjoyment which the soul encounters at every struggle with mankind or with destiny.

These and many other similar thoughts passed through my mind, but I did not follow them up, because I do not like to dwell upon abstract ideas—for what do they lead to? In my early youth I was a dreamer; I loved to hug to my bosom the images—now gloomy, now rainbow-hued—which my restless and eager imagination drew for me. And what is there left to me of all these? Only such weariness as might be felt after a battle by night with a phantom—only a confused memory full of regrets. In that vain contest I have exhausted the warmth of soul and firmness of will indispensable to an active life. I have entered upon that life after having already lived through it in thought, and it has become wearisome and nauseous to me, as the reading of a bad imitation of a book is to one who has long been familiar with the original.

The events of that evening produced a somewhat deep impression upon me and excited my nerves. I do not know for certain whether I now believe in predestination or not, but on that evening I believed in it firmly. The proof was startling, and I, notwithstanding that I had laughed at our forefathers and their obliging astrology, fell involuntarily into their way of thinking. However, I stopped myself in time from following that dangerous road, and, as I have made it a rule not to reject anything decisively and not to trust anything blindly, I cast metaphysics aside and began to look at what was beneath my feet. The precaution was well-timed. I only just escaped stumbling over something thick and soft, but, to all appearance, inanimate. I bent down to see what it was, and, by the light of the moon, which now shone right upon the road, I perceived that it was a pig which had been cut in two with a sabre... I had hardly time to examine it before I heard the sound of steps, and two Cossacks came running out of a byway. One of them came up to me and enquired whether I had seen a drunken Cossack chasing a pig. I informed him that I had not met the Cossack and pointed to the unhappy victim of his rabid bravery.

"The scoundrel!" said the second Cossack. "No sooner does he drink his fill of chikhir [25] than off he goes and cuts up anything that comes in his way. Let us be after him, Eremeich, we must tie him up or else"...

They took themselves off, and I continued my way with greater caution, and at length arrived at my lodgings without mishap.

I was living with a certain old Cossack underofficer whom I loved, not only on account of his kindly disposition, but also, and more especially, on account of his pretty daughter, Nastya.

Wrapped up in a sheepskin coat she was waiting for me, as usual, by the wicket gate. The moon illumined her charming little lips, now turned blue by the cold of the night. Recognizing me she smiled; but I was in no mood to linger with her.

"Good night, Nastya!" I said, and passed on.

She was about to make some answer, but only sighed.

I fastened the door of my room after me, lighted a candle, and threw myself on the bed; but, on that occasion, slumber caused its presence to be awaited longer than usual. By the time I fell asleep the east was beginning to grow pale, but I was evidently predestined not to have my sleep out. At four o'clock in the morning two fists knocked at my window. I sprang up.

"What is the matter?"

"Get up—dress yourself!"

I dressed hurriedly and went out.

"Do you know what has happened?" said three officers who had come for me, speaking all in one voice.

They were deadly pale.

"No, what is it?"

"Vulich has been murdered!"

---

[25] A Caucasian wine.

I was petrified.

"Yes, murdered!" they continued. "Let us lose no time and go!"

"But where to?"

"You will learn as we go."

We set off. They told me all that had happened, supplementing their story with a variety of observations on the subject of the strange predestination which had saved Vulich from imminent death half an hour before he actually met his end.

Vulich had been walking alone along a dark street, and the drunken Cossack who had cut up the pig had sprung out upon him, and perhaps would have passed him by without noticing him, had not Vulich stopped suddenly and said:

"Whom are you looking for, my man?"

"You!" answered the Cossack, striking him with his sabre; and he cleft him from the shoulder almost to the heart...

The two Cossacks who had met me and followed the murderer had arrived on the scene and raised the wounded man from the ground. But he was already as his last gasp and said these three words only—"he was right!"

I alone understood the dark significance of those words: they referred to me. I had involuntarily foretold his fate to poor Vulich. My instinct had not deceived me; I had indeed read on his changed countenance the signs of approaching death.

The murderer had locked himself up in an empty hut at the end of the village; and thither we went. A number of women, all of them weeping, were running in the same direction; at times a belated Cossack, hastily buckling on his dagger, sprang out into the street and overtook us at a run. The tumult was dreadful.

At length we arrived on the scene and found a crowd standing around the hut, the door and shutters of which were locked on the inside. Groups of officers and Cossacks were engaged in heated discussions; the women were shrieking, wailing and talking all in one breath. One of the old women struck my attention by her meaning looks and the frantic despair expressed upon her face. She was sitting on a thick plank, leaning her elbows on her knees and supporting her head with her hands. It was the mother of the murderer. At times her lips moved... Was it a prayer they were whispering, or a curse?

Meanwhile it was necessary to decide upon some course of action and to seize the criminal. Nobody, however, made bold to be the first to rush forward.

I went up to the window and looked in through a chink in the shutter. The criminal, pale of face, was lying on the floor, holding a pistol in his right hand. The blood-stained sabre was beside him. His expressive eyes were rolling in terror; at times he shuddered and clutched at his head, as if indistinctly recalling the events of yesterday. I could not read any sign of great determination in that uneasy glance of his, and I told the major that it would be better at once to give orders to the Cossacks to burst open the door and rush in, than to wait until the murderer had quite recovered his senses.

At that moment the old captain of the Cossacks went up to the door and called the murderer by name. The latter answered back.

"You have committed a sin, brother Ephimych!" said the captain, "so all you can do now is to submit."

"I will not submit!" answered the Cossack.

"Have you no fear of God! You see, you are not one of those cursed Chechenes, but an honest Christian! Come, if you have done it in an unguarded moment there is no help for it! You cannot escape your fate!"

"I will not submit!" exclaimed the Cossack menacingly, and we could hear the snap of the cocked trigger.

"Hey, my good woman!" said the Cossack captain to the old woman. "Say a word to your son—perhaps he will lend an ear to you... You see, to go on like this is only to make God angry. And look, the gentlemen here have already been waiting two hours."

The old woman gazed fixedly at him and shook her head.

"Vasili Petrovich," said the captain, going up to the major; "he will not surrender. I know him! If it comes to smashing in the door he will strike down several of our men. Would it not be better if you ordered him to be shot? There is a wide chink in the shutter."

At that moment a strange idea flashed through my head—like Vulich I proposed to put fate to the test.

"Wait," I said to the major, "I will take him alive."

Bidding the captain enter into a conversation with the murderer and

71

setting three Cossacks at the door ready to force it open and rush to my aid at a given signal, I walked round the hut and approached the fatal window. My heart was beating violently.

"Aha, you cursed wretch!" cried the captain. "Are you laughing at us, eh? Or do you think that we won't be able to get the better of you?"

He began to knock at the door with all his might. Putting my eye to the chink, I followed the movements of the Cossack, who was not expecting an attack from that direction. I pulled the shutter away suddenly and threw myself in at the window, head foremost. A shot rang out right over my ear, and the bullet tore off one of my epaulettes. But the smoke which filled the room prevented my adversary from finding the sabre which was lying beside him. I seized him by the arms; the Cossacks burst in; and three minutes had not elapsed before they had the criminal bound and led off under escort.

The people dispersed, the officers congratulated me—and indeed there was cause for congratulation.

After all that, it would hardly seem possible to avoid becoming a fatalist? But who knows for certain whether he is convinced of anything or not? And how often is a deception of the senses or an error of the reason accepted as a conviction!... I prefer to doubt everything. Such a disposition is no bar to decision of character; on the contrary, so far as I am concerned, I always advance more boldly when I do not know what is awaiting me. You see, nothing can happen worse than death—and from death there is no escape.

On my return to the fortress I related to Maksim Maksimych all that I had seen and experienced; and I sought to learn his opinion on the subject of predestination.

At first he did not understand the word. I explained it to him as well as I could, and then he said, with a significant shake of the head:

"Yes, sir, of course! It was a very ingenious trick! However, these Asiatic pistols often miss fire if they are badly oiled or if you don't press hard enough on the trigger. I confess I don't like the Circassian carbines either. Somehow or other they don't suit the like of us: the butt end is so small, and any minute you may get your nose burnt! On the other hand, their sabres, now—well, all I need say is, my best respects to them!"

Afterwards he said, on reflecting a little:

"Yes, it is a pity about the poor fellow! The devil must have put it into his head to start a conversation with a drunken man at night! However, it is evident that fate had written it so at his birth!"

I could not get anything more out of Maksim Maksimych; generally speaking, he had no liking for metaphysical disputations.

# BOOK V

# THE THIRD EXTRACT FROM PECHORIN'S DIARY

## PRINCESS MARY

### CHAPTER I
### 11th May

YESTERDAY I arrived at Pyatigorsk. I have engaged lodgings at the extreme end of the town, the highest part, at the foot of Mount Mashuk: during a storm the clouds will descend on to the roof of my dwelling.

This morning at five o'clock, when I opened my window, the room was filled with the fragrance of the flowers growing in the modest little front-garden. Branches of bloom-laden bird-cherry trees peep in at my window, and now and again the breeze bestrews my writing-table with their white petals. The view which meets my gaze on three sides is wonderful: westward towers five-peaked Beshtau, blue as "the last cloud of a dispersed storm," [26] and northward rises Mashuk, like a shaggy Persian cap, shutting in the whole of that quarter of the horizon. Eastward the outlook is more cheery: down below are displayed the varied hues of the brand-new, spotlessly clean, little town, with its murmuring, health-giving springs and its babbling, many-tongued throng. Yonder, further away, the mountains tower up in an amphitheatre, ever bluer and mistier; and, at the edge of the horizon, stretches the silver chain of snow-clad summits, beginning with Kazbek and ending with two-peaked Elbruz... Blithe is life in such a land! A feeling akin to rapture is diffused through all my veins. The air is pure and fresh, like the kiss of a child; the sun is bright, the sky is blue—what more

---

[26] Pushkin. Compare Shelley's Adonais, xxxi. 3: "as the last cloud of an expiring storm."

could one possibly wish for? What need, in such a place as this, of passions, desires, regrets?

However, it is time to be stirring. I will go to the Elizaveta spring—I am told that the whole society of the watering-place assembles there in the morning.

Descending into the middle of the town, I walked along the boulevard, on which I met a few melancholy groups slowly ascending the mountain. These, for the most part, were the families of landed-gentry from the steppes—as could be guessed at once from the threadbare, old-fashioned frock-coats of the husbands and the exquisite attire of the wives and daughters. Evidently they already had all the young men of the watering-place at their fingers' ends, because they looked at me with a tender curiosity. The Petersburg cut of my coat misled them; but they soon recognized the military epaulettes, and turned away with indignation.

The wives of the local authorities—the hostesses, so to speak, of the waters—were more graciously inclined. They carry lorgnettes, and they pay less attention to a uniform—they have grown accustomed in the Caucasus to meeting a fervid heart beneath a numbered button and a cultured intellect beneath a white forage-cap. These ladies are very charming, and long continue to be charming. Each year their adorers are exchanged for new ones, and in that very fact, it may be, lies the secret of their unwearying amiability.

Ascending by the narrow path to the Elizaveta spring, I overtook a crowd of officials and military men, who, as I subsequently learned, compose a class apart amongst those who place their hopes in the medicinal waters. They drink—but not water—take but few walks, indulge in only mild flirtations, gamble, and complain of boredom.

They are dandies. In letting their wicker-sheathed tumblers down into the well of sulphurous water they assume academical poses. The officials wear bright blue cravats; the military men have ruffs sticking out above their collars. They affect a profound contempt for provincial ladies, and sigh for the aristocratic drawing-rooms of the capitals—to which they are not admitted.

Here is the well at last!... Upon the small square adjoining it a little house with a red roof over the bath is erected, and somewhat further on there is a gallery in which the people walk when it rains. Some wounded officers were sitting—pale and melancholy—on a bench, with their crutches drawn up. A few ladies, their tumbler of water finished, were walking with rapid steps to and fro about the square. There were two or three pretty faces amongst them. Beneath the avenues of the vines with which the slope of Mashuk is covered, occasional glimpses could be caught of the gay-colored hat of a lover of solitude for two—for beside that hat I always noticed either a military forage-cap or the ugly round hat of a civilian. Upon the steep cliff, where the pavilion called "The Aeolian Harp" is erected, figured the lovers of scenery, directing their telescopes upon Elbruz. Amongst them were a couple of tutors, with their pupils who had come to be cured of scrofula.

Out of breath, I came to a standstill at the edge of the mountain, and, leaning against the corner of a little house, I began to examine the picturesque surroundings, when suddenly I heard behind me a familiar voice.

"Pechorin! Have you been here long?"

I turned round. Grushnitski! We embraced. I had made his acquaintance in the active service detachment. He had been wounded in the foot by a bullet and had come to the waters a week or so before me.

Grushnitski is a cadet; he has only been a year in the service. From a kind of foppery peculiar to himself, he wears the thick cloak of a common soldier. He has also the soldier's cross of St. George. He is well built, swarthy and black-haired. To look at him, you might say he was a man of twenty-five, although he is scarcely twenty-one. He tosses his head when he speaks, and keeps continually twirling his moustache with his left hand, his right hand being occupied with the crutch on which he leans. He speaks rapidly and affectedly; he is one of those people who have a high-sounding phrase ready for every occasion in life, who remain untouched by simple beauty, and who drape themselves majestically in extraordinary sentiments, exalted passions and exceptional sufferings. To produce an effect is their delight; they have an almost insensate fondness for romantic provincial ladies. When old age approaches they become either peaceful landed-gentry or drunkards—sometimes both. Frequently they have many good qualities, but they have not a grain of poetry in their composition. Grushnitski's passion was declamation. He would deluge you with words so soon as the conversation went beyond the sphere of ordinary ideas. I have never been able to dispute with him. He neither answers your questions nor listens to you. So soon as you stop, he begins a lengthy tirade, which has the appearance of being in some sort connected with what you have been saying, but which is, in fact, only a continuation of his own harangue.

He is witty enough; his epigrams are frequently amusing, but never malicious, nor to the point. He slays nobody with a single word; he has no knowledge of men and of their foibles, because all his life he has been interested in nobody but himself. His aim is to make himself the hero of a novel. He has so often endeavored to convince others that he is a being created not for this world and doomed to certain mysterious sufferings,

76

that he has almost convinced himself that such he is in reality. Hence the pride with which he wears his thick soldier's cloak. I have seen through him, and he dislikes me for that reason, although to outward appearance we are on the friendliest of terms. Grushnitski is looked upon as a man of distinguished courage. I have seen him in action. He waves his sabre, shouts, and hurls himself forward with his eyes shut. That is not what I should call Russian courage!...

I reciprocate Grushnitski's dislike. I feel that some time or other we shall come into collision upon a narrow road, and that one of us will fare badly.

His arrival in the Caucasus is also the result of his romantic fanaticism. I am convinced that on the eve of his departure from his paternal village he said with an air of gloom to some pretty neighbor that he was going away, not so much for the simple purpose of serving in the army as of seeking death, because... and hereupon, I am sure, he covered his eyes with his hand and continued thus, "No, you—or thou—must not know! Your pure soul would shudder! And what would be the good? What am I to you? Could you understand me?"... and so on.

He has himself told me that the motive which induced him to enter the K——regiment must remain an everlasting secret between him and Heaven.

However, in moments when he casts aside the tragic mantle, Grushnitski is charming and entertaining enough. I am always interested to see him with women—it is then that he puts forth his finest efforts, I think!

We met like a couple of old friends. I began to question him about the personages of note and as to the sort of life which was led at the waters.

"It is a rather prosaic life," he said, with a sigh. "Those who drink the waters in the morning are inert—like all invalids, and those who drink the wines in the evening are unendurable—like all healthy people! There are ladies who entertain, but there is no great amusement to be obtained from them. They play whist, they dress badly and speak French dreadfully! The only Moscow people here this year are Princess Ligovski and her daughter—but I am not acquainted with them. My soldier's cloak is like a seal of renunciation. The sympathy which it arouses is as painful as charity."

At that moment two ladies walked past us in the direction of the well; one elderly, the other youthful and slender. I could not obtain a good view of their faces on account of their hats, but they were dressed in accordance with the strict rules of the best taste—nothing superfluous. The second lady was wearing a high-necked dress of pearl-grey, and a light silk kerchief was wound round her supple neck. Puce-colored boots clasped her slim little ankle so charmingly, that even those uninitiated into the mysteries of beauty would infallibly have sighed, if only from wonder. There was something maidenly in her easy, but aristocratic gait, something eluding definition yet intelligible to the glance. As she walked past us an indefinable perfume, like that which sometimes breathes from the note of a charming woman, was wafted from her.

"Look!" said Grushnitski, "there is Princess Ligovski with her daughter Mary, as she calls her after the English manner. They have been here only three days."

"You already know her name, though?"

"Yes, I heard it by chance," he answered, with a blush. "I confess I do not desire to make their acquaintance. These haughty aristocrats look upon us army men just as they would upon savages. What care they if there is an intellect beneath a numbered forage-cap, and a heart beneath a thick cloak?"

"Poor cloak!" I said, with a laugh. "But who is the gentleman who is just going up to them and handing them a tumbler so officiously?"

"Oh, that is Raevich, the Moscow dandy. He is a gambler; you can see as much at once from that immense gold chain coiling across his skyblue waistcoat. And what a thick cane he has! Just like Robinson Crusoe's—and so is his beard too, and his hair is done like a peasant's."

"You are embittered against the whole human race?"

"And I have cause to be"...

"Oh, really?"

At that moment the ladies left the well and came up to where we were. Grushnitski succeeded in assuming a dramatic pose with the aid of his crutch, and in a loud tone of voice answered me in French:

"Mon cher, je hais les hommes pour ne pas les mepriser, car autrement la vie serait une farce trop degoutante."

The pretty Princess Mary turned round and favored the orator with a long and curious glance. Her expression was quite indefinite, but it was not contemptuous, a fact on which I inwardly congratulated Grushnitski from my heart.

"She is an extremely pretty girl," I said. "She has such velvet eyes—yes, velvet is the word. I should advise you to appropriate the expression when speaking of her eyes. The lower and upper lashes are so long that the sunbeams are not reflected in her pupils. I love those eyes without a glitter, they are so soft that they appear to caress you. However, her eyes seem to be her only good feature... Tell me, are her teeth white? That is most important! It is a pity that she did not smile at that high-sounding phrase of yours."

"You are speaking of a pretty woman just as you might of an English horse," said Grushnitski indignantly.

"Mon cher," I answered, trying to mimic his tone, "je meprise les femmes, pour ne pas les aimer, car autrement la vie serait un melodrame trop ridicule."

I turned and left him. For half an hour or so I walked about the avenues of the vines, the limestone cliffs and the bushes hanging between them. The day grew hot, and I hurried homewards. Passing the sulphur spring, I stopped at the covered gallery in order to regain my breath under its shade, and by so doing I was afforded the opportunity of witnessing a rather interesting scene. This is the position in which the dramatis personae were disposed: Princess Ligovski and the Moscow dandy were sitting on a bench in the covered gallery—apparently engaged in serious conversation. Princess Mary, who had doubtless by this time finished her last tumbler, was walking pensively to and fro by the well. Grushnitski was standing by the well itself; there was nobody else on the square.

I went up closer and concealed myself behind a corner of the gallery. At that moment Grushnitski let his tumbler fall on the sand and made strenuous efforts to stoop in order to pick it up; but his injured foot prevented him. Poor fellow! How he tried all kinds of artifices, as he leaned on his crutch, and all in vain! His expressive countenance was, in fact, a picture of suffering.

Princess Mary saw the whole scene better than I.

Lighter than a bird she sprang towards him, stooped, picked up the tumbler, and handed it to him with a gesture full of ineffable charm. Then she blushed furiously, glanced round at the gallery, and, having assured herself that her mother apparently had not seen anything, immediately regained her composure. By the time Grushnitski had opened his mouth to thank her she was a long way off. A moment after, she came out of the gallery with her mother and the dandy, but, in passing by Grushnitski, she assumed a most decorous and serious air. She did not even turn round, she did not even observe the passionate gaze which he kept fixed upon her for a long time until she had descended the mountain and was hidden behind the lime trees of the boulevard... Presently I caught glimpses of her hat as she walked along the street. She hurried through the gate of one of the best houses in Pyatigorsk; her mother walked behind her and bowed adieu to Raevich at the gate.

It was only then that the poor, passionate cadet noticed my presence.

"Did you see?" he said, pressing my hand vigorously. "She is an angel, simply an angel!"

"Why?" I inquired, with an air of the purest simplicity.

"Did you not see, then?"

"No. I saw her picking up your tumbler. If there had been an attendant there he would have done the same thing—and quicker too, in the hope of receiving a tip. It is quite easy, however, to understand that she pitied you; you made such a terrible grimace when you walked on the wounded foot."

"And can it be that seeing her, as you did, at that moment when her soul was shining in her eyes, you were not in the least affected?"

"No."

I was lying, but I wanted to exasperate him. I have an innate passion for contradiction—my whole life has been nothing but a series of melancholy and vain contradictions of heart or reason. The presence of an enthusiast chills me with a twelfth-night cold, and I believe that constant association with a person of a flaccid and phlegmatic temperament would have turned me into an impassioned visionary. I confess, too, that an unpleasant but familiar sensation was coursing lightly through my heart at that moment. It was—envy. I say "envy" boldly, because I am accustomed to acknowledge everything to myself. It would be hard to find a young man who, if his idle fancy had been attracted by a pretty woman and he had suddenly found her openly singling out before his eyes another man equally unknown to her—it would be hard, I say, to find such a young man (living, of course, in the great world and accustomed to indulge his self-love) who would not have been unpleasantly taken aback in such a case.

In silence Grushnitski and I descended the mountain and walked along the boulevard, past the windows of the house where our beauty had hidden herself. She was sitting by the window. Grushnitski, plucking me by the arm, cast upon her one of those gloomily tender glances which have so little effect upon women. I directed my lorgnette at her, and observed that she smiled at his glance and that my insolent lorgnette made her downright angry. And how, indeed, should a Caucasian military man presume to direct his eyeglass at a princess from Moscow?...

# CHAPTER II
## 13th May

THIS morning the doctor came to see me. His name is Werner, but he is a Russian. What is there surprising in that? I have known a man named Ivanov, who was a German.

Werner is a remarkable man, and that for many reasons. Like almost all medical men he is a skeptic and a materialist, but, at the same time, he is a genuine poet—a poet always in deeds and often in words, although he has never written two verses in his life. He has mastered all the living chords of the human heart, just as one learns the veins of a corpse, but he has never known how to avail himself of his knowledge. In like manner, it sometimes happens that an excellent anatomist does not know how to cure a fever. Werner usually made fun of his patients in private; but once I saw him weeping over a dying soldier... He was poor, and dreamed of millions, but he would not take a single step out of his way for the sake of money. He once told me that he would rather do a favor to an enemy than to a friend, because, in the latter case, it would mean selling his beneficence, whilst hatred only increases proportionately to the magnanimity of the adversary. He had a malicious tongue; and more than one good, simple soul has acquired the reputation of a vulgar fool through being labelled with one of his epigrams. His rivals, envious medical men of the watering-place, spread the report that he was in the habit of drawing caricatures of his patients. The patients were incensed, and almost all of them discarded him. His friends, that is to say all the genuinely well-bred people who were serving in the Caucasus, vainly endeavored to restore his fallen credit.

His outward appearance was of the type which, at the first glance, creates an unpleasant impression, but which you get to like in course of time, when the eye learns to read in the irregular features the stamp of a tried and lofty soul. Instances have been known of women falling madly in love with men of that sort, and having no desire to exchange their ugliness for the beauty of the freshest and rosiest of Endymions. We must give women their due: they possess an instinct for spiritual beauty, for which reason, possibly, men such as Werner love women so passionately.

Werner was small and lean and as weak as a baby. One of his legs was shorter than the other, as was the case with Byron. In comparison with his body, his head seemed enormous. His hair was cropped close, and the unevennesses of his cranium, thus laid bare, would have struck a phrenologist by reason of the strange intertexture of contradictory propensities. His little, ever restless, black eyes seemed as if they were endeavoring to fathom your thoughts. Taste and neatness were to be observed in his dress. His small, lean, sinewy hands flaunted themselves in bright-yellow gloves. His frock-coat, cravat and waistcoat were invariably of black. The young men dubbed him Mephistopheles; he pretended to be angry at the nickname, but in reality it flattered his vanity. Werner and I soon understood each other and became friends, because I, for my part, am illadapted for friendship. Of two friends, one is always the slave of the other, although frequently neither acknowledges the fact to himself. Now, the slave I could not be; and to be the master would be a wearisome trouble, because, at the same time, deception would be required. Besides, I have servants and money!

Our friendship originated in the following circumstances. I met Werner at S——, in the midst of a numerous and noisy circle of young people. Towards the end of the evening the conversation took a philosophico-metaphysical turn. We discussed the subject of convictions, and each of us had some different conviction to declare.

"So far as I am concerned," said the doctor, "I am convinced of one thing only"...

"And that is—?" I asked, desirous of learning the opinion of a man who had been silent till then.

"Of the fact," he answered, "that sooner or later, one fine morning, I shall die."

"I am better off than you," I said. "In addition to that, I have a further conviction, namely, that, one very nasty evening, I had the misfortune to be born."

All the others considered that we were talking nonsense, but indeed not one of them said anything more sensible. From that moment we singled each other out amongst the crowd. We used frequently to meet and discuss abstract subjects in a very serious manner, until each observed that the other was throwing dust in his eyes. Then, looking significantly at each other—as, according to Cicero, the Roman augurs used to do—we would burst out laughing heartily and, having had our laugh, we would separate, well content with our evening.

I was lying on a couch, my eyes fixed upon the ceiling and my hands clasped behind my head, when Werner entered my room. He sat down in an easy chair, placed his cane in a corner, yawned, and announced that it was getting hot out of doors. I replied that the flies were bothering me—and we both fell silent.

"Observe, my dear doctor," I said, "that, but for fools, the world would be a very dull place. Look! Here are you and I, both sensible men! We know beforehand that it is possible to dispute ad infinitum about everything— and so we do not dispute. Each of us knows almost all the other's secret thoughts: to us a single word is a whole history; we see the grain of every one of our feelings through a threefold husk. What is sad, we laugh at; what is laughable, we grieve at; but, to tell the truth, we are fairly indifferent, generally speaking, to everything except ourselves. Conscquently, there can be no interchange of feelings and thoughts between us; each of us knows all he cares to know about the other, and that knowledge is all he wants. One expedient remains—to tell the news. So tell me some news."

Fatigued by this lengthy speech, I closed my eyes and yawned. The doctor answered after thinking awhile:

"There is an idea, all the same, in that nonsense of yours."

"Two," I replied.

"Tell me one, and I will tell you the other."

"Very well, begin!" I said, continuing to examine the ceiling and smiling inwardly.

"You are anxious for information about some of the new-comers here, and I can guess who it is, because they, for their part, have already been inquiring about you."

"Doctor! Decidedly it is impossible for us to hold a conversation! We read into each other's soul."

"Now the other idea?"...

"Here it is: I wanted to make you relate something, for the following reasons: firstly, listening is less fatiguing than talking; secondly, the listener cannot commit himself; thirdly, he can learn another's secret; fourthly, sensible people, such as you, prefer listeners to speakers. Now to business; what did Princess Ligovski tell you about me?"

"You are quite sure that it was Princess Ligovski... and not Princess Mary?"...

"Quite sure."

"Why?"

"Because Princess Mary inquired about Grushnitski."

"You are gifted with a fine imagination! Princess Mary said that she was convinced that the young man in the soldier's cloak had been reduced to the ranks on account of a duel"...

"I hope you left her cherishing that pleasant delusion"...

"Of course"...

"A plot!" I exclaimed in rapture. "We will make it our business to see to the denouement of this little comedy. It is obvious that fate is taking care that I shall not be bored!"

"I have a presentiment," said the doctor, "that poor Grushnitski will be your victim."

"Proceed, doctor."

"Princess Ligovski said that your face was familiar to her. I observed that she had probably met you in Petersburg—somewhere in society... I told her your name. She knew it well. It appears that your history created a great stir there... She began to tell us of your adventures, most likely supplementing the gossip of society with observations of her own... Her daughter listened with curiosity. In her imagination you have become the hero of a novel in a new style... I did not contradict Princess Ligovski, although I knew that she was talking nonsense."

"Worthy friend!" I said, extending my hand to him.

The doctor pressed it feelingly and continued:

"If you like I will present you"...

"Good heavens!" I said, clapping my hands. "Are heroes ever presented? In no other way do they make the acquaintance of their beloved than by saving her from certain death!"...

"And you really wish to court Princess Mary?"

"Not at all, far from it!... Doctor, I triumph at last! You do not understand me!... It vexes me, however," I continued after a moment's silence. "I never reveal my secrets myself, but I am exceedingly fond of their being guessed, because in that way I can always disavow them upon occasion. However, you must describe both mother and daughter to me. What sort of people are they?"

"In the first place, Princess Ligovski is a woman of forty-five," answered Werner. "She has a splendid digestion, but her blood is out of order—there are red spots on her cheeks. She has spent the latter half of her life in Moscow, and has grown stout from leading an inactive life there. She loves spicy stories, and sometimes says improper things herself when her daughter is out of the room. She has declared to me that her daughter is as innocent as a dove. What does that matter to me?... I was going to answer that she might be at her ease, because I would never tell anyone. Princess Ligovski is taking the cure for her rheumatism, and the daughter, for goodness knows what. I have ordered each of them to drink two tumblers a day of sulphurous water, and to bathe twice a week in the diluted bath. Princess Ligovski is apparently unaccustomed to giving orders. She cherishes respect for the intelligence and attainments of her daughter, who has read Byron in English and knows algebra: in Moscow, evidently, the ladies have entered upon the paths of erudition—and a good thing, too! The men here are generally so unamiable, that, for a clever woman, it must be intolerable to flirt with them. Princess Ligovski is very fond of young people; Princess Mary looks on them with a certain contempt—a Moscow habit! In Moscow they cherish only wits of not less than forty."

"You have been in Moscow, doctor?"

"Yes, I had a practice there."

"Continue."

"But I think I have told everything... No, there is something else: Princess Mary, it seems, loves to discuss emotions, passions, etcetera. She was in Petersburg for one winter, and disliked it—especially the society: no doubt she was coldly received."

"You have not seen anyone with them today?"

"On the contrary, there was an aide-de-camp, a stiff guardsman, and a lady—one of the latest arrivals, a relation of Princess Ligovski on the husband's side—very pretty, but apparently very ill... Have you not met her at the well? She is of medium height, fair, with regular features; she has the complexion of a consumptive, and there is a little black mole on her right cheek. I was struck by the expressiveness of her face."

"A mole!" I muttered through my teeth. "Is it possible?"

The doctor looked at me, and, laying his hand on my heart, said triumphantly:

"You know her!"

My heart was, in fact, beating more violently than usual.

"It is your turn, now, to triumph," I said. "But I rely on you: you will not betray me. I have not seen her yet, but I am convinced that I recognize from your portrait a woman whom I loved in the old days... Do not speak a word to her about me; if she asks any questions, give a bad report of me."

"Be it so!" said Werner, shrugging his shoulders.

When he had departed, my heart was compressed with terrible grief. Has destiny brought us together again in the Caucasus, or has she come hither on purpose, knowing that she would meet me?... And how shall we meet?... And then, is it she?... My presentiments have never deceived me. There is not a man in the world over whom the past has acquired such a power as over me. Every recollection of bygone grief or joy strikes my soul with morbid effect, and draws forth ever the same sounds... I am stupidly constituted: I forget nothing—nothing!

After dinner, about six o'clock, I went on to the boulevard. It was crowded. The two princesses were sitting on a bench, surrounded by young men, who were vying with each other in paying them attention. I took up my position on another bench at a little distance off, stopped two Dragoon officers whom I knew, and proceeded to tell them something. Evidently it was amusing, because they began to laugh loudly like a couple of madmen. Some of those who were surrounding Princess Mary were attracted to my side by curiosity, and gradually all of them left her and joined my circle. I did not stop talking; my anecdotes were clever to the point of absurdity, my jests at the expense of the queer people passing by, malicious to the point of frenzy. I continued to entertain the public till sunset. Princess Mary passed by me a few times, arm-in-arm with her mother, and accompanied by a certain lame old man. A few times her glance as it fell upon me expressed vexation, while endeavoring to express indifference...

"What has he been telling you?" she inquired of one of the young men, who had gone back to her out of politeness. "No doubt a most interesting story—his own exploits in battle?"...

This was said rather loudly, and probably with the intention of stinging me.

"Aha!" I thought to myself. "You are downright angry, my dear Princess. Wait awhile, there is more to follow."

Grushnitski kept following her like a beast of prey, and would not let her out of his sight. I wager that to-morrow he will ask somebody to present him to Princess Ligovski. She will be glad, because she is bored.

# CHAPTER III
# 16th May

IN the course of two days my affairs have gained ground tremendously. Princess Mary positively hates me. Already I have had repeated to me two or three epigrams on the subject of myself—rather caustic, but at the same time very flattering. She finds it exceedingly strange that I, who am accustomed to good society, and am so intimate with her Petersburg cousins and aunts, do not try to make her acquaintance. Every day we meet at the well and on the boulevard. I exert all my powers to entice away her adorers, glittering aides-de-camp, pale-faced visitors from Moscow, and others—and I almost always succeed. I have always hated entertaining guests: now my house is full every day; they dine, sup, gamble, and alas! my champagne triumphs over the might of Princess Mary's magnetic eyes!

I met her yesterday in Chelakhov's shop. She was bargaining for a marvelous Persian rug, and implored her mother not to be niggardly: the rug would be such an ornament to her boudoir... I outbid her by forty rubles, and bought it over her head. I was rewarded with a glance in which the most delightful fury sparkled. About dinnertime, I ordered my Circassian horse, covered with that very rug, purposely to be led past her windows. Werner was with the princesses at the time, and told me that the effect of the scene was most dramatic. Princess Mary wishes to preach a crusade against me, and I have even noticed that, already, two of the aides-de-camp salute me very coldly, when they are in her presence—they dine with me every day, however.

Grushnitski has assumed an air of mystery; he walks with his arms folded behind his back and does not recognize anyone. His foot has got well all at once, and there is hardly a sign of a limp. He has found an opportunity of entering into conversation with Princess Ligovski and of paying Princess Mary some kind of a compliment. The latter is evidently not very fastidious, for, ever since, she answers his bow with a most charming smile.

"Are you sure you do not wish to make the Ligovskis' acquaintance?" he said to me yesterday.

"Positive."

"Good gracious! The pleasantest house at the waters! All the best society of Pyatigorsk is to be found there"...

"My friend, I am terribly tired of even other society than that of Pyatigorsk. So you visit the Ligovskis?"

"Not yet. I have spoken to Princess Mary once or twice, but that is all. You know it is rather awkward to go and visit them without being invited, although that is the custom here... It would be a different matter if I was wearing epaulettes"...

"Good heavens! Why, you are much more interesting as it is! You simply do not know how to avail yourself of your advantageous position... Why, that soldier's cloak makes a hero and a martyr of you in the eyes of any lady of sentiment!"

Grushnitski smiled complacently.

"What nonsense!" he said.

"I am convinced," I continued, "that Princess Mary is in love with you already."

He blushed up to the ears and looked big.

Oh, vanity! Thou art the lever with which Archimedes was to lift the earthly sphere!...

"You are always jesting!" he said, pretending to be angry. "In the first place, she knows so little of me as yet"...

"Women love only those whom they do not know!"

"But I have no pretensions whatsoever to pleasing her. I simply wish to make the acquaintance of an agreeable household; and it would be extremely ridiculous if I were to cherish the slightest hope... With you, now, for instance, it is a different matter! You Petersburg conquerors! You have but to look—and women melt... But do you know, Pechorin, what Princess Mary said of you?"...

"What? She has spoken to you already about me?"...

"Do not rejoice too soon, though. The other day, by chance, I entered into conversation with her at the well; her third word was, 'Who is that gentleman with such an unpleasant, heavy glance? He was with you when'... she blushed, and did not like to mention the day, remembering her own delightful little exploit. 'You need not tell me what day it was,' I answered; 'it will ever be present to my memory!'... Pechorin, my friend, I cannot congratulate you, you are in her black books... And, indeed, it is a pity, because Mary is a charming girl!"...

It must be observed that Grushnitski is one of those men who, in speaking of a woman with whom they are barely acquainted, call her my Mary, my Sophie, if she has had the good fortune to please them.

I assumed a serious air and answered:

"Yes, she is good-looking... Only be careful, Grushnitski! Russian ladies, for the most part, cherish only Platonic love, without mingling any thought of matrimony with it; and Platonic love is exceedingly embarrassing. Princess Mary seems to be one of those women who want to be amused. If she is bored in your company for two minutes on end—you are lost irrevocably. Your silence ought to excite her curiosity, your conversation ought never to satisfy it completely; you should alarm her every minute; ten times, in public, she will slight people's opinion for you and will call that a sacrifice, and, in order to requite herself for it, she will torment you. Afterwards she will simply say that she cannot endure you. If you do not acquire authority over her, even her first kiss will not give you the right to a second. She will flirt with you to her heart's content, and, in two years' time, she will marry a monster, in obedience to her mother, and will assure herself that she is unhappy, that she has loved only one man—that is to say, you—but that Heaven was not willing to unite her to him because he wore a soldier's cloak, although beneath that thick, grey cloak beat a heart, passionate and noble"...

Grushnitski smote the table with his fist and fell to walking to and fro across the room.

I laughed inwardly and even smiled once or twice, but fortunately he did not notice. It is evident that he is in love, because he has grown even more confiding than heretofore. Moreover, a ring has made its appearance on his finger, a silver ring with black enamel of local workmanship. It struck me as suspicious... I began to examine it, and what do you think I saw? The name Mary was engraved on the inside in small letters, and in a line with the name was the date on which she had picked up the famous tumbler. I kept my discovery a secret. I do not want to force confessions from him, I want him, of his own accord, to choose me as his confidant—and then I will enjoy myself!...

To-day I rose late. I went to the well. I found nobody there. The day grew hot. White, shaggy cloudlets were flitting rapidly from the snow-clad mountains, giving promise of a thunderstorm; the summit of Mount Mashuk was smoking like a just extinguished torch; grey wisps of cloud were coiling and creeping like snakes around it, arrested in their rapid sweep and, as it were, hooked to its prickly brushwood. The atmosphere was charged with electricity. I plunged into the avenue of the vines leading to the grotto.

I felt low-spirited. I was thinking of the lady with the little mole on her cheek, of whom the doctor had spoken to me... "Why is she here?" I thought. "And is it she? And what reason have I for thinking it is? And why am I so certain of it? Is there not many a woman with a mole on her cheek?" Reflecting in such wise I came right up to the grotto. I looked in and I saw that a woman, wearing a straw hat and wrapped in a black shawl, was sitting on a stone seat in the cold shade of the arch. Her head was sunk upon her breast, and the hat covered her face. I was just about to turn back, in order not to disturb her meditations, when she glanced at me.

"Vera!" I exclaimed involuntarily.

She started and turned pale.

"I knew that you were here," she said.

I sat down beside her and took her hand. A long-forgotten tremor ran through my veins at the sound of that dear voice. She gazed into my face with her deep, calm eyes. Mistrust and something in the nature of reproach were expressed in her glance.

"We have not seen each other for a long time," I said.

"A long time, and we have both changed in many ways."

"Consequently you love me no longer?"...

"I am married!"... she said.

"Again? A few years ago, however, that reason also existed, but, nevertheless"...

She plucked her hand away from mine and her cheeks flamed.

"Perhaps you love your second husband?"...

She made no answer and turned her head away.

"Or is he very jealous?"

She remained silent.

"What then? He is young, handsome and, I suppose, rich—which is the chief thing—and you are afraid?"...

I glanced at her and was alarmed. Profound despair was depicted upon her countenance; tears were glistening in her eyes.

90

"Tell me," she whispered at length, "do you find it very amusing to torture me? I ought to hate you. Since we have known each other, you have given me naught but suffering"...

Her voice shook; she leaned over to me, and let her head sink upon my breast.

"Perhaps," I reflected, "it is for that very reason that you have loved me; joys are forgotten, but sorrows never"...

I clasped her closely to my breast, and so we remained for a long time. At length our lips drew closer and became blent in a fervent, intoxicating kiss. Her hands were cold as ice; her head was burning.

And hereupon we embarked upon one of those conversations which, on paper, have no sense, which it is impossible to repeat, and impossible even to retain in memory. The meaning of the sounds replaces and completes the meaning of the words, as in Italian opera.

She is decidedly averse to my making the acquaintance of her husband, the lame old man of whom I had caught a glimpse on the boulevard. She married him for the sake of her son. He is rich, and suffers from attacks of rheumatism. I did not allow myself even a single scoff at his expense. She respects him as a father, and will deceive him as a husband... A strange thing, the human heart in general, and woman's heart in particular.

Vera's husband, Semyon Vasilevich G——v, is a distant relation of Princess Ligovski. He lives next door to her. Vera frequently visits the Princess. I have given her my promise to make the Ligovskis' acquaintance, and to pay court to Princess Mary in order to distract attention from Vera. In such way, my plans have been not a little deranged, but it will be amusing for me...

Amusing!... Yes, I have already passed that period of spiritual life when happiness alone is sought, when the heart feels the urgent necessity of violently and passionately loving somebody. Now my only wish is to be loved, and that by very few. I even think that I would be content with one constant attachment. A wretched habit of the heart!...

One thing has always struck me as strange. I have never made myself the slave of the woman I have loved. On the contrary, I have always acquired an invincible power over her will and heart, without in the least endeavoring to do so. Why is this? Is it because I never esteem anything highly, and she has been continually afraid to let me out of her hands? Or is it the magnetic influence of a powerful organism? Or is it, simply, that I have never succeeded in meeting a woman of stubborn character?

I must confess that, in fact, I do not love women who possess strength of character. What business have they with such a thing?

Indeed, I remember now. Once and once only did I love a woman who had a firm will which I was never able to vanquish... We parted as enemies— and then, perhaps, if I had met her five years later we would have parted otherwise...

Vera is ill, very ill, although she does not admit it. I fear she has consumption, or that disease which is called "fievre lente"—a quite unRussian disease, and one for which there is no name in our language.

The storm overtook us while in the grotto and detained us half an hour longer. Vera did not make me swear fidelity, or ask whether I had loved others since we had parted... She trusted in me anew with all her former unconcern, and I will not deceive her: she is the only woman in the world whom it would never be within my power to deceive. I know that we shall soon have to part again, and perchance forever. We will both go by different ways to the grave, but her memory will remain inviolable within my soul. I have always repeated this to her, and she believes me, although she says she does not.

At length we separated. For a long time I followed her with my eyes, until her hat was hidden behind the shrubs and rocks. My heart was painfully contracted, just as after our first parting. Oh, how I rejoiced in that emotion! Can it be that youth is about to come back to me, with its salutary tempests, or is this only the farewell glance, the last gift—in memory of itself?... And to think that, in appearance, I am still a boy! My face, though pale, is still fresh; my limbs are supple and slender; my hair is thick and curly, my eyes sparkle, my blood boils...

Returning home, I mounted on horseback and galloped to the steppe. I love to gallop on a fiery horse through the tall grass, in the face of the desert wind; greedily I gulp down the fragrant air and fix my gaze upon the blue distance, endeavoring to seize the misty outlines of objects which every minute grow clearer and clearer. Whatever griefs oppress my heart, whatever disquietudes torture my thoughts—all are dispersed in a moment; my soul becomes at ease; the fatigue of the body vanquishes the disturbance of the mind. There is not a woman's glance which I would not forget at the sight of the tufted mountains, illumined by the southern sun; at the sight of the dark-blue sky, or in hearkening to the roar of the torrent as it falls from cliff to cliff.

I believe that the Cossacks, yawning on their watch-towers, when they saw me galloping thus needlessly and aimlessly, were long tormented by that enigma, because from my dress, I am sure, they took me to be a Circassian. I have, in fact, been told that when riding on horseback, in my Circassian costume, I resemble a Kabardian more than many a Kabardian himself. And, indeed, so far as regards that noble, warlike garb, I am a perfect dandy. I have not a single piece of gold lace too much; my weapon is costly, but simply wrought; the fur on my cap is neither too long nor too short; my leggings and shoes are matched with all possible accuracy; my tunic is white; my Circassian jacket, dark-brown. I have long studied the mountaineer seat on horseback, and in no way is it possible to flatter my vanity so much as by acknowledging my skill in horsemanship in the Cossack mode. I keep four horses—one for myself and three for my friends, so that I may not be bored by having to roam about the fields all alone; they take my horses with pleasure, and never ride with me.

It was already six o'clock in the evening, when I remembered that it was time to dine. My horse was jaded. I rode out on to the road leading from Pyatigorsk to the German colony, to which the society of the watering-place frequently rides en piquenique. The road meanders between bushes and descends into little ravines, through which flow noisy brooks beneath the shade of tall grasses. All around, in an amphitheatre, rise the blue masses of Mount Beshtau and the Zmeiny, Zhelezny and Lysy Mountains.[27] Descending into one of those ravines, I halted to water my horse. At that moment a noisy and glittering cavalcade made its appearance upon the road—the ladies in black and dark-blue riding habits, the cavaliers in costumes which formed a medley of the Circassian and Nizhegorodian. [28] In front rode Grushnitski with Princess Mary.

The ladies at the watering-place still believe in attacks by Circassians in broad daylight; for that reason, doubtless, Grushnitski had slung a sabre and a pair of pistols over his soldier's cloak. He looked ridiculous enough in that heroic attire.

I was concealed from their sight by a tall bush, but I was able to see everything through the leaves, and to guess from the expression of their faces that the conversation was of a sentimental turn. At length they approached the slope; Grushnitski took hold of the bridle of the Princess's horse, and then I heard the conclusion of their conversation:

"And you wish to remain all your life in the Caucasus?" said Princess Mary.

"What is Russia to me?" answered her cavalier. "A country in which thousands of people, because they are richer than I, will look upon me with contempt, whilst here—here this thick cloak has not prevented my acquaintance with you"...

"On the contrary"... said Princess Mary, blushing.

---

[27] The Snake, the Iron and the Bald Mountains.
[28] Nizhegorod is the "government" of which Nizhniy Novgorod is the capital.

Grushnitski's face was a picture of delight. He continued:

"Here, my life will flow along noisily, unobserved, and rapidly, under the bullets of the savages, and if Heaven were every year to send me a single bright glance from a woman's eyes—like that which—"

At that moment they came up to where I was. I struck my horse with the whip and rode out from behind the bush...

"Mon Dieu, un circassien!"... exclaimed Princess Mary in terror.

In order completely to undeceive her, I replied in French, with a slight bow:

"Ne craignez rien, madame, je ne suis pas plus dangereux que votre cavalier"...

She grew embarrassed—but at what? At her own mistake, or because my answer struck her as insolent? I should like the latter hypothesis to be correct. Grushnitski cast a discontented glance at me.

Late in the evening, that is to say, about eleven o'clock, I went for a walk in the lilac avenue of the boulevard. The town was sleeping; lights were gleaming in only a few windows. On three sides loomed the black ridges of the cliffs, the spurs of Mount Mashuk, upon the summit of which an ominous cloud was lying. The moon was rising in the east; in the distance, the snow-clad mountains glistened like a fringe of silver. The calls of the sentries mingled at intervals with the roar of the hot springs let flow for the night. At times the loud clattering of a horse rang out along the street, accompanied by the creaking of a Nagai wagon and the plaintive burden of a Tartar song.

I sat down upon a bench and fell into a reverie... I felt the necessity of pouring forth my thoughts in friendly conversation... But with whom?...

"What is Vera doing now?" I wondered.

I would have given much to press her hand at that moment.

All at once I heard rapid and irregular steps... Grushnitski, no doubt!... So it was!

"Where have you come from?"

"From Princess Ligovski's," he said very importantly. "How well Mary does sing!"...

94

"Do you know?" I said to him. "I wager that she does not know that you are a cadet. She thinks you are an officer reduced to the ranks"...

"Maybe so. What is that to me!"... he said absently.

"No, I am only saying so"...

"But, do you know that you have made her terribly angry to-day? She considered it an unheard-of piece of insolence. It was only with difficulty that I was able to convince her that you are so well bred and know society so well that you could not have had any intention of insulting her. She says that you have an impudent glance, and that you have certainly a very high opinion of yourself."

"She is not mistaken... But do you not want to defend her?"

"I am sorry I have not yet the right to do so"...

"Oho!" I said to myself, "evidently he has hopes already."

"However, it is the worse for you," continued Grushnitski; "it will be difficult for you to make their acquaintance now, and what a pity! It is one of the most agreeable houses I know"...

I smiled inwardly.

"The most agreeable house to me now is my own," I said, with a yawn, and I got up to go.

"Confess, though, you repent?"...

"What nonsense! If I like I will be at Princess Ligovski's to-morrow evening!"...

"We shall see"...

"I will even begin to pay my addresses to Princess Mary, if you would like me to"...

"Yes, if she is willing to speak to you"...

"I am only awaiting the moment when she will be bored by your conversation... Goodbye"...

"Well, I am going for a stroll; I could not go to sleep now for anything... Look here, let us go to the restaurant instead, there is cardplaying going on there... What I need now is violent sensations"...

"I hope you will lose"...

I went home.

# CHAPTER IV
## 21st May

NEARLY a week has passed, and I have not yet made the Ligovskis' acquaintance. I am awaiting a convenient opportunity. Grushnitski follows Princess Mary everywhere like a shadow. Their conversations are interminable; but, when will she be tired of him?... Her mother pays no attention, because he is not a man who is in a position to marry. Behold the logic of mothers! I have caught two or three tender glances—this must be put a stop to.

Yesterday, for the first time, Vera made her appearance at the well... She has never gone out of doors since we met in the grotto. We let down our tumblers at the same time, and as she bent forward she whispered to me:

"You are not going to make the Ligovskis' acquaintance?... It is only there that wc can meet"...

A reproach!... How tiresome! But I have deserved it...

By the way, there is a subscription ball tomorrow in the saloon of the restaurant, and I will dance the mazurka with Princess Mary.

# CHAPTER V
## 29th May

THE saloon of the restaurant was converted into the assembly room of a Nobles' Club. The company met at nine o'clock. Princess Ligovski and her daughter were amongst the latest to make their appearance. Several of the ladies looked at Princess Mary with envy and malevolence, because she dresses with taste. Those who look upon themselves as the aristocracy of the place concealed their envy and attached themselves to her train. What else could be expected? Wherever there is a gathering of women, the company is immediately divided into a higher and a lower circle.

Beneath the window, amongst a crowd of people, stood Grushnitski, pressing his face to the pane and never taking his eyes off his divinity. As she passed by, she gave him a hardly perceptible nod. He beamed like the sun... The first dance was a polonaise, after which the musicians struck up a waltz. Spurs began to jingle, and skirts to rise and whirl.

I was standing behind a certain stout lady who was overshadowed by rose-colored feathers. The magnificence of her dress reminded me of the times of the farthingale, and the motley hue of her by no means smooth skin, of the happy epoch of the black taffeta patch. An immense wart on her neck was covered by a clasp. She was saying to her cavalier, a captain of dragoons:

"That young Princess Ligovski is a most intolerable creature! Just fancy, she jostled against me and did not apologise, but even turned round and stared at me through her lorgnette!... C'est impayable!... And what has she to be proud of? It is time somebody gave her a lesson"...

"That will be easy enough," replied the obliging captain, and he directed his steps to the other room.

I went up to Princess Mary immediately, and, availing myself of the local customs which allowed one to dance with a stranger, I invited her to waltz with me.

She was scarcely able to keep from smiling and letting her triumph be seen; but quickly enough she succeeded in assuming an air of perfect indifference and even severity. Carelessly she let her hand fall upon my shoulder, inclined her head slightly to one side, and we began to dance. I have never known a waist more voluptuous and supple! Her fresh breath touched my face; at times a lock of hair, becoming separated from its companions in the eddy of the waltz, glided over my burning cheek...

I made three turns of the ballroom (she waltzes surprisingly well). She was out of breath, her eyes were dulled, her half-open lips were scarcely able to whisper the indispensable: "merci, monsieur."

After a few moments' silence I said to her, assuming a very humble air:

"I have heard, Princess, that although quite unacquainted with you, I have already had the misfortune to incur your displeasure... that you have considered me insolent. Can that possibly true?"

"Would you like to confirm me in that opinion now?" she answered, with an ironical little grimace—very becoming, however, to her mobile countenance.

"If I had the audacity to insult you in any way, then allow me to have the still greater audacity to beg your pardon... And, indeed, I should very much like to prove to you that you are mistaken in regard to me"...

"You will find that a rather difficult task"...

"But why?"...

"Because you never visit us and, most likely, there will not be many more of these balls."

"That means," I thought, "that their doors are closed to me forever."

"You know, Princess," I said to her, with a certain amount of vexation, "one should never spurn a penitent criminal: in his despair he may become twice as much a criminal as before... and then"...

Sudden laughter and whispering from the people around us caused me to turn my head and to interrupt my phrase. A few paces away from me stood a group of men, amongst them the captain of dragoons, who had manifested intentions hostile to the charming Princess. He was particularly well pleased with something or other, and was rubbing his hands, laughing and exchanging meaning glances with his companions. All at once a gentleman in an evening-dress coat and with long moustaches and a red face separated himself from the crowd and directed his uncertain steps straight towards Princess Mary. He was drunk. Coming to a halt opposite the embarrassed Princess and placing his hands behind his back, he fixed his dull grey eyes upon her, and said in a hoarse treble:

"Permettez... but what is the good of that sort of thing here... All I need say is: I engage you for the mazurka"...

"Very well!" she replied in a trembling voice, throwing a beseeching glance around. Alas! Her mother was a long way off, and not one of the cavaliers of her acquaintance was near. A certain aide-de-camp apparently saw the whole scene, but he concealed himself behind the crowd in order not to be mixed up in the affair.

"What?" said the drunken gentleman, winking to the captain of dragoons, who was encouraging him by signs. "Do you not wish to dance then?... All the same I again have the honor to engage you for the mazurka... You think, perhaps, that I am drunk! That is all right!... I can dance all the easier, I assure you"...

98

I saw that she was on the point of fainting with fright and indignation.

I went up to the drunken gentleman, caught him none too gently by the arm, and, looking him fixedly in the face, requested him to retire. "Because," I added, "the Princess promised long ago to dance the mazurka with me."

"Well, then, there's nothing to be done! Another time!" he said, bursting out laughing, and he retired to his abashed companions, who immediately conducted him into another room.

I was rewarded by a deep, wondrous glance.

The Princess went up to her mother and told her the whole story. The latter sought me out among the crowd and thanked me. She informed me that she knew my mother and was on terms of friendship with half a dozen of my aunts.

"I do not know how it has happened that we have not made your acquaintance up to now," she added; "but confess, you alone are to blame for that. You fight shy of everyone in a positively unseemly way. I hope the air of my drawingroom will dispel your spleen... Do you not think so?"

I uttered one of the phrases which everybody must have ready for such an occasion.

The quadrilles dragged on a dreadfully long time.

At last the music struck up from the gallery, Princess Mary and I took up our places.

I did not once allude to the drunken gentleman, or to my previous behavior, or to Grushnitski. The impression produced upon her by the unpleasant scene was gradually dispelled; her face brightened up; she jested very charmingly; her conversation was witty, without pretensions to wit, vivacious and spontaneous; her observations were sometimes profound... In a very involved sentence I gave her to understand that I had liked her for a long time. She bent her head and blushed slightly.

"You are a strange man!" she said, with a forced laugh, lifting her velvet eyes upon me.

"I did not wish to make your acquaintance," I continued, "because you are surrounded by too dense a throng of adorers, in which I was afraid of being lost to sight altogether."

"You need not have been afraid; they are all very tiresome"...

99

"All? Not all, surely?"

She looked fixedly at me as if endeavoring to recollect something, then blushed slightly again and finally pronounced with decision:

"All!"

"Even my friend, Grushnitski?"

"But is he your friend?" she said, manifesting some doubt.

"Yes."

"He, of course, does not come into the category of the tiresome"...

"But into that of the unfortunate!" I said, laughing.

"Of course! But do you consider that funny? I should like you to be in his place"...

"Well? I was once a cadet myself, and, in truth, it was the best time of my life!"

"Is he a cadet, then?"... she said rapidly, and then added: "But I thought"...

"What did you think?"...

"Nothing! Who is that lady?"

Thereupon the conversation took a different direction, and it did not return to the former subject.

And now the mazurka came to an end and we separated—until we should meet again. The ladies drove off in different directions. I went to get some supper, and met Werner.

"Aha!" he said: "so it is you! And yet you did not wish to make the acquaintance of Princess Mary otherwise than by saving her from certain death."

"I have done better," I replied. "I have saved her from fainting at the ball"...

"How was that? Tell me."

"No, guess!—O, you who guess everything in the world!"

# CHAPTER VI
## 30th May

ABOUT seven o'clock in the evening, I was walking on the boulevard. Grushnitski perceived me a long way off, and came up to me. A sort of ridiculous rapture was shining in his eyes. He pressed my hand warmly, and said in a tragic voice:

"I thank you, Pechorin... You understand me?"

"No; but in any case it is not worth gratitude," I answered, not having, in fact, any good deed upon my conscience.

"What? But yesterday! Have you forgotten?... Mary has told me everything"...

"Why! Have you everything in common so soon as this? Even gratitude?"...

"Listen," said Grushnitski very earnestly; "pray do not make fun of my love, if you wish to remain my friend... You see, I love her to the point of madness... and I think—I hope—she loves me too... I have a request to make of you. You will be at their house this evening; promise me to observe everything. I know you are experienced in these matters, you know women better than I... Women! Women! Who can understand them? Their smiles contradict their glances, their words promise and allure, but the tone of their voice repels... At one time they grasp and divine in a moment our most secret thoughts, at another they cannot understand the clearest hints... Take Princess Mary, now: yesterday her eyes, as they rested upon me, were blazing with passion; to-day they are dull and cold"...

"That is possibly the result of the waters," I replied.

"You see the bad side of everything... materialist," he added contemptuously. "However, let us talk of other matters."

And, satisfied with his bad pun, he cheered up.

At nine o'clock we went to Princess Ligovski's together.

Passing by Vera's windows, I saw her looking out. We threw a fleeting glance at each other. She entered the Ligovskis' drawing-room soon after us. Princess Ligovski presented me to her, as a relation of her own. Tea was served. The guests were numerous, and the conversation was general. I endeavored to please the Princess, jested, and made her laugh heartily a few times. Princess Mary, also, was more than once on the point of bursting out laughing, but she restrained herself in order not to depart from the role she had assumed. She finds languor becoming to her, and perhaps she is not mistaken. Grushnitski appears to be very glad that she is not infected by my gaiety.

After tea we all went into the drawingroom.

"Are you satisfied with my obedience, Vera?" I said as I was passing her.

She threw me a glance full of love and gratitude. I have grown accustomed to such glances; but at one time they constituted my felicity. The Princess seated her daughter at the pianoforte, and all the company begged her to sing. I kept silence, and, taking advantage of the hubbub, I went aside to the window with Vera, who wished to say something of great importance to both of us... It turned out to be—nonsense...

Meanwhile my indifference was vexing Princess Mary, as I was able to make out from a single angry, gleaming glance which she cast at me... Oh! I understand the method of conversation wonderfully well: mute but expressive, brief but forceful!...

She began to sing. She has a good voice, but she sings badly... However, I was not listening.

Grushnitski, on the contrary, leaning his elbows on the grand piano, facing her, was devouring her with his eyes and saying in an undertone every minute: "Charmant! Delicieux!"

"Listen," said Vera to me, "I do not wish you to make my husband's acquaintance, but you must, without fail, make yourself agreeable to the Princess; that will be an easy task for you: you can do anything you wish. It is only here that we shall see each other"...

"Only here?"...

She blushed and continued:

"You know that I am your slave: I have never been able to resist you... and I shall be punished for it, you will cease to love me! At least, I want to preserve my reputation... not for myself—that you know very well!... Oh! I beseech you: do not torture me, as before, with idle doubts and feigned coldness! It may be that I shall die soon; I feel that I am growing weaker from day to day... And, yet, I cannot think of the future life, I think only of you... You men do not understand the delights of a glance, of a pressure of the hand... but as for me, I swear to you that, when I listen to your voice, I feel such a deep, strange bliss that the most passionate kisses could not take its place."

Meanwhile, Princess Mary had finished her song. Murmurs of praise were to be heard all around. I went up to her after all the other guests, and said something rather carelessly to her on the subject of her voice.

She made a little grimace, pouting her lower lip, and dropped a very sarcastic curtsey.

"That is all the more flattering," she said, "because you have not been listening to me at all; but perhaps you do not like music?"...

"On the contrary, I do... After dinner, especially."

"Grushnitski is right in saying that you have very prosaic tastes... and I see that you like music in a gastronomic respect."

"You are mistaken again: I am by no means an epicure. I have a most wretched digestion. But music after dinner puts one to sleep, and to sleep after dinner is healthful; consequently I like music in a medicinal respect. In the evening, on the contrary, it excites my nerves too much: I become either too melancholy or too gay. Both are fatiguing, where there is no positive reason for being either sorrowful or glad. And, moreover, melancholy in society is ridiculous, and too great gaiety is unbecoming"...

She did not hear me to the end, but went away and sat beside Grushnitski, and they entered into a sort of sentimental conversation. Apparently the Princess answered his sage phrases rather absent-mindedly and inconsequently, although endeavoring to show that she was listening to him with attention, because sometimes he looked at her in astonishment, trying to divine the cause of the inward agitation which was expressed at times in her restless glance...

But I have found you out, my dear Princess! Have a care! You want to pay me back in the same coin, to wound my vanity—you will not succeed! And if you declare war on me, I will be merciless!

In the course of the evening, I purposely tried a few times to join in their conversation, but she met my remarks rather coldly, and, at last, I retired in pretended vexation. Princess Mary was triumphant, Grushnitski likewise. Triumph, my friends, and be quick about it!... You will not have long to triumph!... It cannot be otherwise. I have a presentiment... On making a woman's acquaintance I have always unerringly guessed whether she would fall in love with me or not.

The remaining part of the evening I spent at Vera's side, and talked to the full about the old days... Why does she love me so much? In truth, I am unable to say, all the more so because she is the only woman who has understood me perfectly, with all my petty weaknesses and evil passions... Can it be that wickedness is so attractive?...

Grushnitski and I left the house together. In the street he took my arm, and, after a long silence, said:

"Well?"

"You are a fool," I should have liked to answer. But I restrained myself and only shrugged my shoulders.

# CHAPTER VII
# 6th June

ALL these days I have not once departed from my system. Princess Mary has come to like talking to me; I have told her a few of the strange events of my life, and she is beginning to look on me as an extraordinary man. I mock at everything in the world, especially feelings; and she is taking alarm. When I am present, she does not dare to embark upon sentimental discussions with Grushnitski, and already, on a few occasions, she has answered his sallies with a mocking smile. But every time that Grushnitski comes up to her I assume an air of meekness and leave the two of them together. On the first occasion, she was glad, or tried to make it appear so; on the second, she was angry with me; on the third—with Grushnitski.

"You have very little vanity!" she said to me yesterday. "What makes you think that I find Grushnitski the more entertaining?"

I answered that I was sacrificing my own pleasure for the sake of the happiness of a friend.

"And my pleasure, too," she added.

I looked at her intently and assumed a serious air. After that for the whole day I did not speak a single word to her... In the evening, she was pensive; this morning, at the well, more pensive still. When I went up to her, she was listening absent-mindedly to Grushnitski, who was apparently falling into raptures about Nature, but, so soon as she perceived me, she began to laugh—at a most inopportune moment—pretending not to notice me. I went on a little further and began stealthily to observe her. She turned away from her companion and yawned twice. Decidedly she had grown tired of Grushnitski—I will not talk to her for another two days.

# CHAPTER VIII
# 11th June

I OFTEN ask myself why I am so obstinately endeavoring to win the love of a young girl whom I do not wish to deceive, and whom I will never marry. Why this woman-like coquetry? Vera loves me more than Princess Mary ever will. Had I regarded the latter as an invincible beauty, I should perhaps have been allured by the difficulty of the undertaking...

However, there is no such difficulty in this case! Consequently, my present feeling is not that restless craving for love which torments us in the early days of our youth, flinging us from one woman to another until we find one who cannot endure us. And then begins our constancy—that sincere, unending passion which may be expressed mathematically by a line falling from a point into space—the secret of that endlessness lying only in the impossibility of attaining the aim, that is to say, the end.

From what motive, then, am I taking all this trouble?—Envy of Grushnitski? Poor fellow!

He is quite undeserving of it. Or, is it the result of that ugly, but invincible, feeling which causes us to destroy the sweet illusions of our neighbor in order to have the petty satisfaction of saying to him, when, in despair, he asks what he is to believe:

"My friend, the same thing happened to me, and you see, nevertheless, that I dine, sup, and sleep very peacefully, and I shall, I hope, know how to die without tears and lamentations."

There is, in sooth, a boundless enjoyment in the possession of a young, scarce-budded soul! It is like a floweret which exhales its best perfume at the kiss of the first ray of the sun. You should pluck the flower at that moment, and, breathing its fragrance to the full, cast it upon the road: perchance someone will pick it up! I feel within me that insatiate hunger which devours everything it meets upon the way; I look upon the sufferings and joys of others only from the point of view of their relation to myself, regarding them as the nutriment which sustains my spiritual forces. I myself am no longer capable of committing follies under the influence of passion; with me, ambition has been repressed by circumstances, but it has emerged in another form, because ambition is nothing more nor less than a thirst for power, and my chief pleasure is to make everything that surrounds me subject to my will. To arouse the feeling of love, devotion and awe towards oneself—is not that the first sign, and the greatest triumph, of power? To be the cause of suffering and joy to another—without in the least possessing any definite right to be so—is not that the sweetest food for our pride? And what is happiness?—Satisfied pride. Were I to consider myself the best, the most powerful man in the world, I should be happy; were all to love me, I should find within me inexhaustible springs of love. Evil begets evil; the first suffering gives us the conception of the satisfaction of torturing another. The idea of evil cannot enter the mind without arousing a desire to put it actually into practice. "Ideas are organic entities," someone has said. The very fact of their birth endows them with form, and that form is action. He in whose brain the most ideas are born accomplishes the most. From that cause a genius, chained to an official desk, must die or go mad, just as it often happens that a man of powerful constitution, and at the same time of sedentary life and simple habits, dies of an apoplectic stroke.

Passions are naught but ideas in their first development; they are an attribute of the youth of the heart, and foolish is he who thinks that he will be agitated by them all his life. Many quiet rivers begin their course as noisy waterfalls, and there is not a single stream which will leap or foam throughout its way to the sea. That quietness, however, is frequently the sign of great, though latent, strength. The fullness and depth of feelings and thoughts do not admit of frenzied outbursts. In suffering and in enjoyment the soul renders itself a strict account of all it experiences and convinces itself that such things must be. It knows that, but for storms, the constant heat of the sun would dry it up! It imbues itself with its own life—pets and punishes itself like a favorite child. It is only in that highest state of self-knowledge that a man can appreciate the divine justice.

On reading over this page, I observe that I have made a wide digression from my subject... But what matter?... You see, it is for myself that I am writing this diary, and, consequently anything that I jot down in it will in time be a valuable reminiscence for me.

Grushnitski has called to see me to-day. He flung himself upon my neck; he has been promoted to be an officer. We drank champagne. Doctor Werner came in after him.

"I do not congratulate you," he said to Grushnitski.

"Why not?"

"Because the soldier's cloak suits you very well, and you must confess that an infantry uniform, made by one of the local tailors, will not add anything of interest to you... Do you not see? Hitherto, you have been an exception, but now you will come under the general rule."

"Talk away, doctor, talk away! You will not prevent me from rejoicing. He does not know," added Grushnitski in a whisper to me, "how many hopes these epaulettes have lent me... Oh!... Epaulettes, epaulettes! Your little stars are guiding stars! No! I am perfectly happy now!"

"Are you coming with us on our walk to the hollow?" I asked him.

"I? Not on any account will I show myself to Princess Mary until my uniform is finished."

"Would you like me to inform her of your happiness?"

"No, please, not a word... I want to give her a surprise"...

"Tell me, though, how are you getting on with her?"

He became embarrassed, and fell into thought; he would gladly have bragged and told lies, but his conscience would not let him; and, at the same time, he was ashamed to confess the truth.

"What do you think? Does she love you?"...

"Love me? Good gracious, Pechorin, what ideas you do have!... How could she possibly love me so soon?... And a well-bred woman, even if she is in love, will never say so"...

"Very well! And, I suppose, in your opinion, a well-bred man should also keep silence in regard to his passion?"...

"Ah, my dear fellow! There are ways of doing everything; often things may remain unspoken, but yet may be guessed"...

"That is true... But the love which we read in the eyes does not pledge a woman to anything, whilst words... Have a care, Grushnitski, she is befooling you!"

"She?" he answered, raising his eyes heavenward and smiling complacently. "I am sorry for you, Pechorin!"...

He took his departure.

In the evening, a numerous company set off to walk to the hollow.

In the opinion of the learned of Pyatigorsk, the hollow in question is nothing more nor less than an extinct crater. It is situated on a slope of Mount Mashuk, at the distance of a verst from the town, and is approached by a narrow path between brushwood and rocks. In climbing up the hill, I gave Princess Mary my arm, and she did not leave it during the whole excursion.

Our conversation commenced with slander; I proceeded to pass in review our present and absent acquaintances; at first I exposed their ridiculous, and then their bad, sides. My choler rose. I began in jest, and ended in genuine malice. At first she was amused, but afterwards frightened.

"You are a dangerous man!" she said. "I would rather perish in the woods under the knife of an assassin than under your tongue... In all earnestness I beg of you: when it comes into your mind to speak evil of me, take a knife instead and cut my throat. I think you would not find that a very difficult matter."

"Am I like an assassin, then?"...

"You are worse"...

I fell into thought for a moment; then, assuming a deeply moved air, I said:

"Yes, such has been my lot from very childhood! All have read upon my countenance the marks of bad qualities, which were not existent; but they were assumed to exist—and they were born. I was modest—I was accused of slyness: I grew secretive. I profoundly felt both good and evil—no one caressed me, all insulted me: I grew vindictive. I was gloomy—other children merry and talkative; I felt myself higher than they—I was rated lower: I grew envious. I was prepared to love the whole world—no one understood me: I learned to hate. My colorless youth flowed by in conflict with myself and the world; fearing ridicule, I buried my best feelings in the depths of my heart, and there they died. I spoke the truth—I was not believed: I began to deceive. Having acquired a thorough knowledge of the world and the springs of society, I grew skilled in the science of life; and I saw how others without skill were happy, enjoying gratuitously the advantages which I so unweariedly sought. Then despair was born within my breast—not that despair which is cured at the muzzle of a pistol, but the cold, powerless despair concealed beneath the mask of amiability and a good-natured smile. I became a moral cripple. One half of my soul ceased to exist; it dried up, evaporated, died, and I cut it off and cast it from me. The other half moved and lived—at the service of all; but it remained unobserved, because no one knew that the half which had perished had ever existed. But, now, the memory of it has been awakened within me by you, and I have read you its epitaph. To many, epitaphs in general seem ridiculous, but to me they do not; especially when I remember what reposes beneath them. I will not, however, ask you to share my opinion. If this outburst seems absurd to you, I pray you, laugh! I forewarn you that your laughter will not cause me the least chagrin."

At that moment I met her eyes: tears were welling in them. Her arm, as it leaned upon mine, was trembling; her cheeks were aflame; she pitied me! Sympathy—a feeling to which all women yield so easily, had dug its talons into her inexperienced heart. During the whole excursion she was preoccupied, and did not flirt with anyone—and that is a great sign!

We arrived at the hollow; the ladies left their cavaliers, but she did not let go my arm. The witticisms of the local dandies failed to make her laugh; the steepness of the declivity beside which she was standing caused her no alarm, although the other ladies uttered shrill cries and shut their eyes.

On the way back, I did not renew our melancholy conversation, but to my idle questions and jests she gave short and absent-minded answers.

"Have you ever been in love?" I asked her at length.

She looked at me intently, shook her head and again fell into a reverie. It was evident that she was wishing to say something, but did not know how to begin. Her breast heaved... And, indeed, that was but natural! A muslin sleeve is a weak protection, and an electric spark was running from my arm to hers. Almost all passions have their beginning in that way, and frequently we are very much deceived in thinking that a woman loves us for our moral and physical merits; of course, these prepare and predispose the heart for the reception of the holy flame, but for all that it is the first touch that decides the matter.

"I have been very amiable to-day, have I not?" Princess Mary said to me, with a forced smile, when we had returned from the walk.

We separated.

She is dissatisfied with herself. She accuses herself of coldness... Oh, that is the first, the chief triumph!

To-morrow, she will be feeling a desire to recompense me. I know the whole proceeding by heart already—that is what is so tiresome!

# CHAPTER IX
## 12th June

I HAVE seen Vera to-day. She has begun to plague me with her jealousy. Princess Mary has taken it into her head, it seems, to confide the secrets of her heart to Vera: a happy choice, it must be confessed!

"I can guess what all this is leading to," said Vera to me. "You had better simply tell me at once that you are in love with her."

"But supposing I am not in love with her?"

"Then why run after her, disturb her, agitate her imagination!... Oh, I know you well! Listen—if you wish me to believe you, come to Kislovodsk in a week's time; we shall be moving thither the day after to-morrow. Princess Mary will remain here longer. Engage lodgings next door to us. We shall be living in the large house near the spring, on the mezzanine floor. Princess Ligovski will be below us, and next door there is a house belonging to the same landlord, which has not yet been taken... Will you come?"...

I gave my promise, and this very same day I have sent to engage the lodgings.

Grushnitski came to me at six o'clock and announced that his uniform would be ready to-morrow, just in time for him to go to the ball in it.

"At last I shall dance with her the whole evening through... And then I shall talk to my heart's content," he added.

"When is the ball?"

"Why, to-morrow! Do you not know, then? A great festival—and the local authorities have undertaken to organize it"...

"Let us go to the boulevard"...

"Not on any account, in this nasty cloak"...

"What! Have you ceased to love it?"...

I went out alone, and, meeting Princess Mary I asked her to keep the mazurka for me. She seemed surprised and delighted.

"I thought that you would only dance from necessity as on the last occasion," she said, with a very charming smile...

She does not seem to notice Grushnitski's absence at all.

"You will be agreeably surprised to-morrow," I said to her.

"At what?"

"That is a secret... You will find it out yourself, at the ball."

I finished up the evening at Princess Ligovski's; there were no other guests present except Vera and a certain very amusing, little old gentleman. I was in good spirits, and improvised various extraordinary stories. Princess Mary sat opposite me and listened to my nonsense with such deep, strained, and even tender attention that I grew ashamed of myself. What had become of her vivacity, her coquetry, her caprices, her haughty mien, her contemptuous smile, her absentminded glance?...

Vera noticed everything, and her sickly countenance was a picture of profound grief. She was sitting in the shadow by the window, buried in a wide arm-chair... I pitied her.

Then I related the whole dramatic story of our acquaintanceship, our love—concealing it all, of course, under fictitious names.

So vividly did I portray my tenderness, my anxieties, my raptures; in so favorable a light did I exhibit her actions and her character, that involuntarily she had to forgive me for my flirtation with Princess Mary.

She rose, sat down beside us, and brightened up... and it was only at two o'clock in the morning that we remembered that the doctors had ordered her to go to bed at eleven.

# CHAPTER X
## 13th June

HALF an hour before the ball, Grushnitski presented himself to me in the full splendor of the uniform of the Line infantry. Attached to his third button was a little bronze chain, on which hung a double lorgnette. Epaulettes of incredible size were bent backwards and upwards in the shape of a cupid's wings; his boots creaked; in his left hand he held cinnamon-colored kid gloves and a forage-cap, and with his right he kept every moment twisting his frizzled tuft of hair up into tiny curls. Complacency and at the same time a certain diffidence were depicted upon his face. His festal appearance and proud gait would have made me burst out laughing, if such a proceeding had been in accordance with my intentions.

He threw his cap and gloves on the table and began to pull down the skirts of his coat and to put himself to rights before the looking-glass. An enormous black handkerchief, which was twisted into a very high stiffener for his cravat, and the bristles of which supported his chin, stuck out an inch over his collar. It seemed to him to be rather small, and he drew it up as far as his ears. As a result of that hard work—the collar of his uniform being very tight and uncomfortable—he grew red in the face.

"They say you have been courting my princess terribly these last few days?" he said, rather carelessly and without looking at me.

"'Where are we fools to drink tea!'" [29] I answered, repeating a pet phrase of one of the cleverest rogues of past times, once celebrated in song by Pushkin. "Tell me, does my uniform fit me well?... Oh, the cursed Jew!... How it cuts me under the armpits!... Have you got any scent?"

"Good gracious, what more do you want? You are reeking of rose pomade as it is."

"Never mind. Give me some"...

He poured half a phial over his cravat, his pocket-handkerchief, his sleeves.

"You are going to dance?" he asked.

"I think not."

"I am afraid I shall have to lead off the mazurka with Princess Mary, and I scarcely know a single figure"...

"Have you asked her to dance the mazurka with you?"

"Not yet"...

"Mind you are not forestalled"...

---

[29] A popular phrase, equivalent to: "How should I think of doing such a thing?"

"Just so, indeed!" he said, striking his forehead. "Good-bye... I will go and wait for her at the entrance."

He seized his forage-cap and ran.

Half an hour later I also set off. The street was dark and deserted. Around the assembly rooms, or inn—whichever you prefer—people were thronging. The windows were lighted up, the strains of the regimental band were borne to me on the evening breeze. I walked slowly; I felt melancholy.

"Can it be possible," I thought, "that my sole mission on earth is to destroy the hopes of others? Ever since I began to live and to act, it seems always to have been my fate to play a part in the ending of other people's dramas, as if, but for me, no one could either die or fall into despair! I have been the indispensable person of the fifth act; unwillingly I have played the pitiful part of an executioner or a traitor. What object has fate had in this?... Surely, I have not been appointed by destiny to be an author of middle-class tragedies and family romances, or to be a collaborator with the purveyor of stories—for the 'Reader's Library,' [30] for example?... How can I tell?... Are there not many people who, in beginning life, think to end it like Lord Byron or Alexander the Great, and, nevertheless, remain Titular Councillors [31] all their days?"

Entering the saloon, I concealed myself in a crowd of men, and began to make my observations.

Grushnitski was standing beside Princess Mary and saying something with great warmth. She was listening to him absent-mindedly and looking about her, her fan laid to her lips. Impatience was depicted upon her face, her eyes were searching all around for somebody. I went softly behind them in order to listen to their conversation.

"You torture me, Princess!" Grushnitski was saying. "You have changed dreadfully since I saw you last"...

"You, too, have changed," she answered, casting a rapid glance at him, in which he was unable to detect the latent sneer.

"I! Changed?... Oh, never! You know that such a thing is impossible! Whoever has seen you once will bear your divine image with him forever."

"Stop"...

---

[30] Published by Senkovski, and under the censorship of the Government.

[31] Civil servants of the ninth (the lowest) class.

"But why will you not let me say to-night what you have so often listened to with condescension—and just recently, too?"...

"Because I do not like repetitions," she answered, laughing.

"Oh! I have been bitterly mistaken!... I thought, fool that I was, that these epaulettes, at least, would give me the right to hope... No, it would have been better for me to have remained forever in that contemptible soldier's cloak, to which, probably, I was indebted for your attention"...

"As a matter of fact, the cloak is much more becoming to you"...

At that moment I went up and bowed to Princess Mary. She blushed a little, and went on rapidly:

"Is it not true, Monsieur Pechorin, that the grey cloak suits Monsieur Grushnitski much better?"...

"I do not agree with you," I answered: "he is more youthful-looking still in his uniform."

That was a blow which Grushnitski could not bear: like all boys, he has pretensions to being an old man; he thinks that the deep traces of passions upon his countenance take the place of the lines scored by Time. He cast a furious glance at me, stamped his foot, and took himself off.

"Confess now," I said to Princess Mary: "that although he has always been most ridiculous, yet not so long ago he seemed to you to be interesting... in the grey cloak?"...

She cast her eyes down and made no reply.

Grushnitski followed the Princess about during the whole evening and danced either with her or vis-a-vis. He devoured her with his eyes, sighed, and wearied her with prayers and reproaches. After the third quadrille she had begun to hate him.

"I did not expect this from you," he said, coming up to me and taking my arm.

"What?"

"You are going to dance the mazurka with her?" he asked in a solemn tone. "She admitted it"...

"Well, what then? It is not a secret, is it"?

114

"Of course not... I ought to have expected such a thing from that chit—that flirt... I will have my revenge, though!"

"You should lay the blame on your cloak, or your epaulettes, but why accuse her? What fault is it of hers that she does not like you any longer?"...

"But why give me hopes?"

"Why did you hope? To desire and to strive after something—that I can understand! But whoever hopes?"

"You have won the wager, but not quite," he said, with a malignant smile.

The mazurka began. Grushnitski chose no one but the Princess, other cavaliers chose her every minute: obviously a conspiracy against me—all the better! She wants to talk to me, they are preventing her—she will want to twice as much.

I squeezed her hand once or twice; the second time she drew it away without saying a word.

"I shall sleep badly to-night," she said to me when the mazurka was over.

"Grushnitski is to blame for that."

"Oh, no!"

And her face became so pensive, so sad, that I promised myself that I would not fail to kiss her hand that evening.

The guests began to disperse. As I was handing Princess Mary into her carriage, I rapidly pressed her little hand to my lips. The night was dark and nobody could see.

I returned to the saloon very well satisfied with myself.

The young men, Grushnitski amongst them, were having supper at the large table. As I came in, they all fell silent: evidently they had been talking about me. Since the last ball many of them have been sulky with me, especially the captain of dragoons; and now, it seems, a hostile gang is actually being formed against me, under the command of Grushnitski. He wears such a proud and courageous air...

I am very glad; I love enemies, though not in the Christian sense. They amuse me, stir my blood. To be always on one's guard, to catch every glance, the meaning of every word, to guess intentions, to crush

115

conspiracies, to pretend to be deceived and suddenly with one blow to overthrow the whole immense and laboriously constructed edifice of cunning and design—that is what I call life.

During supper Grushnitski kept whispering and exchanging winks with the captain of dragoons.

# CHAPTER XI
## 14th June

VERA and her husband left this morning for Kislovodsk. I met their carriage as I was walking to Princess Ligovski's. Vera nodded to me: reproach was in her glance.

Who is to blame, then? Why will she not give me an opportunity of seeing her alone? Love is like fire—if not fed it dies out. Perchance, jealousy will accomplish what my entreaties have failed to do.

I stayed a whole hour at Princess Ligovski's. Mary has not been out, she is ill. In the evening she was not on the boulevard. The newly formed gang, armed with lorgnettes, has in very fact assumed a menacing aspect. I am glad that Princess Mary is ill; they might be guilty of some impertinence towards her. Grushnitski goes about with dishevelled locks, and wears an appearance of despair: he is evidently afflicted, as a matter of fact; his vanity especially has been injured. But, you see, there are some people in whom even despair is diverting!...

On my way home I noticed that something was lacking. I have not seen her! She is ill! Surely I have not fallen in love with her in real earnest?... What nonsense!

# CHAPTER XII
## 15th June

AT eleven o'clock in the morning—the hour at which Princess Ligovski is usually perspiring in the Ermolov baths—I walked past her house. Princess Mary was sitting pensively at the window; on seeing me she sprang up.

I entered the ante-room, there was nobody there, and, availing myself of the freedom afforded by the local customs, I made my way, unannounced, into the drawing-room.

Princess Mary's charming countenance was shrouded with a dull pallor. She was standing by the pianoforte, leaning one hand on the back of an arm-chair; her hand was very faintly trembling. I went up to her softly and said:

"You are angry with me?"...

She lifted a deep, languid glance upon me and shook her head. Her lips were about to utter something, but failed; her eyes filled with tears; she sank into the arm-chair and buried her face in her hands.

"What is the matter with you?" I said, taking her hand.

"You do not respect me!... Oh, leave me!"...

I took a few steps... She drew herself up in the chair, her eyes sparkled.

I stopped still, took hold of the handle of the door, and said:

"Forgive me, Princess. I have acted like a madman... It will not happen another time; I shall see to that... But how can you know what has been taking place hitherto within my soul? That you will never learn, and so much the better for you. Farewell."

As I was going out, I seemed to hear her weeping.

I wandered on foot about the environs of Mount Mashuk till evening, fatigued myself terribly and, on arriving home, flung myself on my bed, utterly exhausted.

Werner came to see me.

"Is it true," he asked, "that you are going to marry Princess Mary?"

"What?"

"The whole town is saying so. All my patients are occupied with that important piece of news; but you know what these patients are: they know everything."

"This is one of Grushnitski's tricks," I said to myself.

"To prove the falsity of these rumours, doctor, I may mention, as a secret, that I am moving to Kislovodsk to-morrow"...

"And Princess Mary, too?"

"No, she remains here another week"...

"So you are not going to get married?"...

"Doctor, doctor! Look at me! Am I in the least like a bridegroom, or any such thing?"

"I am not saying so... But you know there are occasions..." he added, with a crafty smile—"in which an honorable man is obliged to marry, and there are mothers who, to say the least, do not prevent such occasions... And so, as a friend, I should advise you to be more cautious. The air of these parts is very dangerous. How many handsome young men, worthy of a better fate, have I not seen departing from here straight to the altar!... Would you believe me, they were even going to find a wife for me! That is to say, one person was—a lady belonging to this district, who had a very pale daughter. I had the misfortune to tell her that the latter's color would be restored after wedlock, and then with tears of gratitude she offered me her daughter's hand and the whole of her own fortune—fifty souls, [32] I think. But I replied that I was unfit for such an honor."

Werner left, fully convinced that he had put me on my guard.

I gathered from his words that various ugly rumours were already being spread about the town on the subject of Princess Mary and myself: Grushnitski shall smart for this!

# CHAPTER XIII
# 18th June

I HAVE been in Kislovodsk three days now. Every day I see Vera at the well and out walking. In the morning, when I awake, I sit by my window and direct my lorgnette at her balcony. She has already been dressed long ago, and is waiting for the signal agreed upon. We meet, as though unexpectedly, in the garden which slopes down from our houses to the well. The life-giving mountain air has brought back her color and her strength. Not for nothing is Narzan called the "Spring of Heroes." The inhabitants aver that the air of Kislovodsk predisposes the heart to love and that all the romances which have had their beginning at the foot of Mount Mashuk find their consummation here. And, in very fact,

---

[32] i.e. serfs.

everything here breathes of solitude; everything has an air of secrecy—the thick shadows of the linden avenues, bending over the torrent which falls, noisy and foaming, from flag to flag and cleaves itself a way between the mountains now becoming clad with verdure—the mist-filled, silent ravines, with their ramifications straggling away in all directions—the freshness of the aromatic air, laden with the fragrance of the tall southern grasses and the white acacia—the never-ceasing, sweetly-slumberous babble of the cool brooks, which, meeting at the end of the valley, flow along in friendly emulation, and finally fling themselves into the Podkumok. On this side, the ravine is wider and becomes converted into a verdant dell, through which winds the dusty road. Every time I look at it, I seem to see a carriage coming along and a rosy little face looking out of the carriage-window. Many carriages have already driven by—but still there is no sign of that particular one. The village which lies behind the fortress has become populous. In the restaurant, built upon a hill a few paces distant from my lodgings, lights are beginning to flash in the evening through the double row of poplars; noise and the jingling of glasses resound till late at night.

In no place are such quantities of Kakhetian wine and mineral waters drunk as here.

"And many are willing to mix the two,

But that is a thing I never do."

Every day Grushnitski and his gang are to be found brawling in the inn, and he has almost ceased to greet me.

He only arrived yesterday, and has already succeeded in quarrelling with three old men who were going to take their places in the baths before him.

Decidedly, his misfortunes are developing a warlike spirit within him.

# CHAPTER XIV
## 22nd June

AT last they have arrived. I was sitting by the window when I heard the clattering of their carriage. My heart throbbed... What does it mean? Can it be that I am in love?... I am so stupidly constituted that such a thing might be expected of me.

I dined at their house. Princess Ligovski looked at me with much tenderness, and did not leave her daughter's side... a bad sign! On the other hand, Vera is jealous of me in regard to Princess Mary—however, I have been striving for that good fortune. What will not a woman do in order to chagrin her rival? I remember that once a woman loved me simply because I was in love with another woman. There is nothing more paradoxical than the female mind; it is difficult to convince a woman of anything; they have to be led into convincing themselves. The order of the proofs by which they demolish their prejudices is most original; to learn their dialectic it is necessary to overthrow in your own mind every scholastic rule of logic. For example, the usual way:

"This man loves me; but I am married: therefore I must not love him."

The woman's way:

"I must not love him, because I am married; but he loves me—therefore"...

A few dots here, because reason has no more to say. But, generally, there is something to be said by the tongue, and the eyes, and, after these, the heart—if there is such a thing.

What if these notes should one day meet a woman's eye?

"Slander!" she will exclaim indignantly.

Ever since poets have written and women have read them (for which the poets should be most deeply grateful) women have been called angels so many times that, in very truth, in their simplicity of soul, they have believed the compliment, forgetting that, for money, the same poets have glorified Nero as a demigod...

It would be unreasonable were I to speak of women with such malignity—I who have loved nothing else in the world—I who have always been ready to sacrifice for their sake ease, ambition, life itself... But, you see, I am not endeavoring, in a fit of vexation and injured vanity, to pluck from them the magic veil through which only an accustomed glance can penetrate. No, all that I say about them is but the result of

"A mind which coldly hath observed,

A heart which bears the stamp of woe." [33]

Women ought to wish that all men knew them as well as I because I have loved them a hundred times better since I have ceased to be afraid of them and have comprehended their little weaknesses.

---

[33] Pushkin: Eugene Onyegin.

By the way: the other day, Werner compared women to the enchanted forest of which Tasso tells in his "Jerusalem Delivered." [34]

"So soon as you approach," he said, "from all directions terrors, such as I pray Heaven may preserve us from, will take wing at you: duty, pride, decorum, public opinion, ridicule, contempt... You must simply go straight on without looking at them; gradually the monsters disappear, and, before you, opens a bright and quiet glade, in the midst of which blooms the green myrtle. On the other hand, woe to you if, at the first steps, your heart trembles and you turn back!"

# CHAPTER XV
## 24th June

THIS evening has been fertile in events. About three versts from Kislovodsk, in the gorge through which the Podkumok flows, there is a cliff called the Ring. It is a naturally formed gate, rising upon a lofty hill, and through it the setting sun throws its last flaming glance upon the world. A numerous cavalcade set off thither to gaze at the sunset through the rock-window. To tell the truth, not one of them was thinking about the sun. I rode beside Princess Mary. On the way home, we had to ford the Podkumok. Mountain streams, even the smallest, are dangerous; especially so, because the bottom is a perfect kaleidoscope: it changes every day owing to the pressure of the current; where yesterday there was a rock, to-day there is a cavity. I took Princess Mary's horse by the bridle and led it into the water, which came no higher than its knees. We began to move slowly in a slanting direction against the current. It is a well-known fact that, in crossing rapid streamlets, you should never look at the water, because, if you do, your head begins to whirl directly. I forgot to warn Princess Mary of that.

We had reached the middle and were right in the vortex, when suddenly she reeled in her saddle.

"I feel ill!" she said in a faint voice.

I bent over to her rapidly and threw my arm around her supple waist.

"Look up!" I whispered. "It is nothing; just be brave! I am with you."

---

[34] Canto XVIII, 10:
   "Quinci al bosco t' invia, dove cotanti
   Son fantasmi inganne vole e bugiardi"...

She grew better; she was about to disengage herself from my arm, but I clasped her tender, soft figure in a still closer embrace; my cheek almost touched hers, from which was wafted flame.

"What are you doing to me?... Oh, Heaven!"...

I paid no attention to her alarm and confusion, and my lips touched her tender cheek. She shuddered, but said nothing. We were riding behind the others: nobody saw us.

When we made our way out on the bank, the horses were all put to the trot. Princess Mary kept hers back; I remained beside her. It was evident that my silence was making her uneasy, but I swore to myself that I would not speak a single word—out of curiosity. I wanted to see how she would extricate herself from that embarrassing position.

"Either you despise me, or you love me very much!" she said at length, and there were tears in her voice. "Perhaps you want to laugh at me, to excite my soul and then to abandon me... That would be so base, so vile, that the mere supposition... Oh, no!" she added, in a voice of tender trustfulness; "there is nothing in me which would preclude respect; is it not so? Your presumptuous action... I must, I must forgive you for it, because I permitted it... Answer, speak, I want to hear your voice!"...

There was such womanly impatience in her last words that, involuntarily, I smiled; happily it was beginning to grow dusk... I made no answer.

"You are silent!" she continued; "you wish, perhaps, that I should be the first to tell you that I love you."...

I remained silent.

"Is that what you wish?" she continued, turning rapidly towards me.... There was something terrible in the determination of her glance and voice.

"Why?" I answered, shrugging my shoulders.

She struck her horse with her riding-whip and set off at full gallop along the narrow, dangerous road. It all happened so quickly that I was scarcely able to overtake her, and then only by the time she had joined the rest of the company.

All the way home she was continually talking and laughing. There was something feverish in her movements; not once did she look in my direction. Everybody observed her unusual gaiety. Princess Ligovski rejoiced inwardly as she looked at her daughter. However, the latter simply has a fit of nerves: she will spend a sleepless night, and will weep.

This thought affords me measureless delight: there are moments when I understand the Vampire... And yet I am reputed to be a good fellow, and I strive to earn that designation!

On dismounting, the ladies went into Princess Ligovski's house. I was excited, and I galloped to the mountains in order to dispel the thoughts which had thronged into my head. The dewy evening breathed an intoxicating coolness. The moon was rising from behind the dark summits. Each step of my unshod horse resounded hollowly in the silence of the gorges. I watered the horse at the waterfall, and then, after greedily inhaling once or twice the fresh air of the southern night.

I set off on my way back. I rode through the village. The lights in the windows were beginning to go out; the sentries on the fortress-rampart and the Cossacks in the surrounding pickets were calling out in drawling tones to one another.

In one of the village houses, built at the edge of a ravine, I noticed an extraordinary illumination. At times, discordant murmurs and shouting could be heard, proving that a military carouse was in full swing. I dismounted and crept up to the window. The shutter had not been made fast, and I could see the banqueters and catch what they were saying. They were talking about me.

The captain of dragoons, flushed with wine, struck the table with his fist, demanding attention.

"Gentlemen!" he said, "this won't do! Pechorin must be taught a lesson! These Petersburg fledglings always carry their heads high until they get a slap in the face! He thinks that because he always wears clean gloves and polished boots he is the only one who has ever lived in society. And what a haughty smile! All the same, I am convinced that he is a coward—yes, a coward!"

"I think so too," said Grushnitski. "He is fond of getting himself out of trouble by pretending to be only having a joke. I once gave him such a talking to that anyone else in his place would have cut me to pieces on the spot. But Pechorin turned it all to the ridiculous side. I, of course, did not call him out because that was his business, but he did not care to have anything more to do with it."

"Grushnitski is angry with him for having captured Princess Mary from him," somebody said.

"That's a new idea! It is true I did run after Princess Mary a little, but I left off at once because I do not want to get married; and it is against my rules to compromise a girl."

123

"Yes, I assure you that he is a coward of the first water, I mean Pechorin, not Grushnitski—but Grushnitski is a fine fellow, and, besides, he is my true friend!" the captain of dragoons went on.

"Gentlemen! Nobody here stands up for him? Nobody? So much the better! Would you like to put his courage to the test? It would be amusing"...

"We would; but how?"

"Listen here, then: Grushnitski in particular is angry with him—therefore to Grushnitski falls the chief part. He will pick a quarrel over some silly trifle or other, and will challenge Pechorin to a duel... Wait a bit; here is where the joke comes in... He will challenge him to a duel; very well! The whole proceeding—challenge, preparations, conditions—will be as solemn and awe-inspiring as possible—I will see to that. I will be your second, my poor friend! Very well! Only here is the rub; we will put no bullets in the pistols. I can answer for it that Pechorin will turn coward—I will place them six paces apart, devil take it! Are you agreed, gentlemen?"

"Splendid idea!... Agreed!... And why not?"... came from all sides.

"And you, Grushnitski?"

Tremblingly I awaited Grushnitski's answer. I was filled with cold rage at the thought that, but for an accident, I might have made myself the laughing-stock of those fools. If Grushnitski had not agreed, I should have thrown myself upon his neck; but, after an interval of silence, he rose from his place, extended his hand to the captain, and said very gravely:

"Very well, I agree!"

It would be difficult to describe the enthusiasm of that honorable company.

I returned home, agitated by two different feelings. The first was sorrow.

"Why do they all hate me?" I thought—"why? Have I affronted anyone? No. Can it be that I am one of those men the mere sight of whom is enough to create animosity?"

And I felt a venomous rage gradually filling my soul.

"Have a care, Mr. Grushnitski!" I said, walking up and down the room: "I am not to be jested with like this! You may pay dearly for the approbation of your foolish comrades. I am not your toy!"...

124

I got no sleep that night. By daybreak I was as yellow as an orange.

In the morning I met Princess Mary at the well.

"You are ill?" she said, looking intently at me.

"I did not sleep last night."

"Nor I either... I was accusing you... perhaps groundlessly. But explain yourself, I can forgive you everything"...

"Everything?"...

"Everything... only speak the truth... and be quick... You see, I have been thinking a good deal, trying to explain, to justify, your behavior. Perhaps you are afraid of opposition on the part of my relations... that will not matter. When they learn"...

Her voice shook.

"I will win them over by entreaties. Or, is it your own position?... But you know that I can sacrifice everything for the sake of the man I love... Oh, answer quickly—have pity... You do not despise me—do you?"

She seized my hand.

Princess Ligovski was walking in front of us with Vera's husband, and had not seen anything; but we might have been observed by some of the invalids who were strolling about—the most inquisitive gossips of all inquisitive folk—and I rapidly disengaged my hand from her passionate pressure.

"I will tell you the whole truth," I answered. "I will not justify myself, nor explain my actions: I do not love you."

Her lips grew slightly pale.

"Leave me," she said, in a scarcely audible voice.

I shrugged my shoulders, turned round, and walked away.

# CHAPTER XVI
## 25th June

I SOMETIMES despise myself... Is not that the reason why I despise others also?... I have grown incapable of noble impulses; I am afraid of appearing ridiculous to myself. In my place, another would have offered Princess Mary son coeur et sa fortune; but over me the word "marry" has a kind of magical power. However passionately I love a woman, if she only gives me to feel that I have to marry her—then farewell, love! My heart is turned to stone, and nothing will warm it anew. I am prepared for any other sacrifice but that; my life twenty times over, nay, my honor I would stake on the fortune of a card... but my freedom I will never sell. Why do I prize it so highly? What is there in it to me? For what am I preparing myself? What do I hope for from the future?... In truth, absolutely nothing. It is a kind of innate dread, an inexplicable prejudice... There are people, you know, who have an unaccountable dread of spiders, beetles, mice... Shall I confess it? When I was but a child, a certain old woman told my fortune to my mother. She predicted for me death from a wicked wife. I was profoundly struck by her words at the time: an irresistible repugnance to marriage was born within my soul... Meanwhile, something tells me that her prediction will be realized; I will try, at all events, to arrange that it shall be realized as late in life as possible.

# CHAPTER XVII
## 26th June

YESTERDAY, the conjurer Apfelbaum arrived here. A long placard made its appearance on the door of the restaurant, informing the most respected public that the above-mentioned marvelous conjurer, acrobat, chemist, and optician would have the honor to give a magnificent performance on the present day at eight o'clock in the evening, in the saloon of the Nobles' Club (in other words, the restaurant); tickets—two rubles and a half each.

Everyone intends to go and see the marvelous conjurer; even Princess Ligovski has taken a ticket for herself, in spite of her daughter being ill.

After dinner to-day, I walked past Vera's windows; she was sitting by herself on the balcony. A note fell at my feet:

"Come to me at ten o'clock this evening by the large staircase. My husband has gone to Pyatigorsk and will not return before to-morrow morning. My servants and maids will not be at home; I have distributed tickets to all of them, and to the princess's servants as well. I await you; come without fail."

"Aha!" I said to myself, "so then it has turned out at last as I thought it would."

At eight o'clock I went to see the conjurer. The public assembled before the stroke of nine. The performance began. On the back rows of chairs I recognized Vera's and Princess Ligovski's menservants and maids. They were all there, every single one. Grushnitski, with his lorgnette, was sitting in the front row, and the conjurer had recourse to him every time he needed a handkerchief, a watch, a ring and so forth.

For some time past, Grushnitski has ceased to bow to me, and to-day he has looked at me rather insolently once or twice. It will all be remembered to him when we come to settle our scores.

Before ten o'clock had struck, I stood up and went out.

It was dark outside, pitch dark. Cold, heavy clouds were lying on the summit of the surrounding mountains, and only at rare intervals did the dying breeze rustle the tops of the poplars which surrounded the restaurant. People were crowding at the windows. I went down the mountain and, turning in under the gate, I hastened my pace. Suddenly it seemed to me that somebody was following my steps. I stopped and looked round. It was impossible to make out anything in the darkness. However, out of caution, I walked round the house, as if taking a stroll. Passing Princess Mary's windows, I again heard steps behind me; a man wrapped in a cloak ran by me. That rendered me uneasy, but I crept up to the flight of steps, and hastily mounted the dark staircase. A door opened, and a little hand seized mine...

"Nobody has seen you?" said Vera in a whisper, clinging to me.

"Nobody."

"Now do you believe that I love you? Oh! I have long hesitated, long tortured myself... But you can do anything you like with me."

Her heart was beating violently, her hands were cold as ice. She broke out into complaints and jealous reproaches. She demanded that I should confess everything to her, saying that she would bear my faithlessness with submission, because her sole desire was that I should be happy. I did not quite believe that, but I calmed her with oaths, promises and so on.

"So you will not marry Mary? You do not love her?... But she thinks... Do you know, she is madly in love with you, poor girl!"...

127

About two o'clock in the morning I opened the window and, tying two shawls together, I let myself down from the upper balcony to the lower, holding on by the pillar. A light was still burning in Princess Mary's room. Something drew me towards that window. The curtain was not quite drawn, and I was able to cast a curious glance into the interior of the room. Mary was sitting on her bed, her hands crossed upon her knees; her thick hair was gathered up under a lace-frilled nightcap; her white shoulders were covered by a large crimson kerchief, and her little feet were hidden in a pair of many-colored Persian slippers. She was sitting quite still, her head sunk upon her breast; on a little table in front of her was an open book; but her eyes, fixed and full of inexpressible grief, seemed for the hundredth time to be skimming the same page whilst her thoughts were far away.

At that moment somebody stirred behind a shrub. I leaped from the balcony on to the sward. An invisible hand seized me by the shoulder.

"Aha!" said a rough voice: "caught!... I'll teach you to be entering princesses' rooms at night!"

"Hold him fast!" exclaimed another, springing out from a corner.

It was Grushnitski and the captain of dragoons.

I struck the latter on the head with my fist, knocked him off his feet, and darted into the bushes. All the paths of the garden which covered the slope opposite our houses were known to me.

"Thieves, guard!"... they cried.

A gunshot rang out; a smoking wad fell almost at my feet.

Within a minute I was in my own room, undressed and in bed. My manservant had only just locked the door when Grushnitski and the captain began knocking for admission.

"Pechorin! Are you asleep? Are you there?"... cried the captain.

"I am in bed," I answered angrily.

"Get up! Thieves!... Circassians!"...

"I have a cold," I answered. "I am afraid of catching a chill."

They went away. I had gained no useful purpose by answering them: they would have been looking for me in the garden for another hour or so.

Meanwhile the alarm became terrific. A Cossack galloped up from the fortress. The commotion was general; Circassians were looked for in every shrub—and of course none were found. Probably, however, a good many people were left with the firm conviction that, if only more courage and dispatch had been shown by the garrison, at least a score of brigands would have failed to get away with their lives.

# CHAPTER XVIII
## 27th June

THIS morning, at the well, the sole topic of conversation was the nocturnal attack by the Circassians. I drank the appointed number of glasses of Narzan water, and, after sauntering a few times about the long linden avenue, I met Vera's husband, who had just arrived from Pyatigorsk. He took my arm and we went to the restaurant for breakfast. He was dreadfully uneasy about his wife.

"What a terrible fright she had last night," he said. "Of course, it was bound to happen just at the very time when I was absent."

We sat down to breakfast near the door leading into a corner-room in which about a dozen young men were sitting. Grushnitski was amongst them. For the second time destiny provided me with the opportunity of overhearing a conversation which was to decide his fate. He did not see me, and, consequently, it was impossible for me to suspect him of design; but that only magnified his fault in my eyes.

"Is it possible, though, that they were really Circassians?" somebody said. "Did anyone see them?"

"I will tell you the whole truth," answered Grushnitski: "only please do not betray me. This is how it was: yesterday, a certain man, whose name I will not tell you, came up to me and told me that, at ten o'clock in the evening, he had seen somebody creeping into the Ligovskis' house. I must observe that Princess Ligovski was here, and Princess Mary at home. So he and I set off to wait beneath the windows and waylay the lucky man."

I confess I was frightened, although my companion was very busily engaged with his breakfast: he might have heard things which he would have found rather displeasing, if Grushnitski had happened to guess the truth; but, blinded by jealousy, the latter did not even suspect it.

"So, do you see?" Grushnitski continued. "We set off, taking with us a gun, loaded with blank cartridge, so as just to give him a fright. We waited in the garden till two o'clock. At length—goodness knows, indeed, where he appeared from, but he must have come out by the glass door which is behind the pillar; it was not out of the window that he came, because the window had remained unopened—at length, I say, we saw someone getting down from the balcony... What do you think of Princess Mary—eh? Well, I admit, it is hardly what you might expect from Moscow ladies! After that what can you believe? We were going to seize him, but he broke away and darted like a hare into the shrubs. Thereupon I fired at him."

There was a general murmur of incredulity.

"You do not believe it?" he continued. "I give you my word of honor as a gentleman that it is all perfectly true, and, in proof, I will tell you the man's name if you like."

"Tell us, tell us, who was he?" came from all sides.

"Pechorin," answered Grushnitski.

At that moment he raised his eyes—I was standing in the doorway opposite to him. He grew terribly red. I went up to him and said, slowly and distinctly:

"I am very sorry that I did not come in before you had given your word of honor in confirmation of a most abominable calumny: my presence would have saved you from that further act of baseness."

Grushnitski jumped up from his seat and seemed about to fly into a passion.

"I beg you," I continued in the same tone: "I beg you at once to retract what you have said; you know very well that it is all an invention. I do not think that a woman's indifference to your brilliant merits should deserve so terrible a revenge. Bethink you well: if you maintain your present attitude, you will lose the right to the name of gentleman and will risk your life."

Grushnitski stood before me in violent agitation, his eyes cast down. But the struggle between his conscience and his vanity was of short duration. The captain of dragoons, who was sitting beside him, nudged him with his elbow. Grushnitski started, and answered rapidly, without raising his eyes:

"My dear sir, what I say, I mean, and I am prepared to repeat... I am not afraid of your menaces and am ready for anything."

"The latter you have already proved," I answered coldly; and, taking the captain of dragoons by the arm, I left the room.

130

"What do you want?" asked the captain.

"You are Grushnitski's friend and will no doubt be his second?"

The captain bowed very gravely.

"You have guessed rightly," he answered.

"Moreover, I am bound to be his second, because the insult offered to him touches myself also. I was with him last night," he added, straightening up his stooping figure.

"Ah! So it was you whose head I struck so clumsily?"...

He turned yellow in the face, then blue; suppressed rage was portrayed upon his countenance.

"I shall have the honor to send my second to you to-day," I added, bowing adieu to him very politely, without appearing to have noticed his fury.

On the restaurant-steps I met Vera's husband. Apparently he had been waiting for me.

He seized my hand with a feeling akin to rapture.

"Noble young man!" he said, with tears in his eyes. "I have heard everything. What a scoundrel! Ingrate!... Just fancy such people being admitted into a decent household after this! Thank God I have no daughters! But she for whom you are risking your life will reward you. Be assured of my constant discretion," he continued. "I have been young myself and have served in the army: I know that these affairs must take their course. Good-bye."

Poor fellow! He is glad that he has no daughters!...

I went straight to Werner, found him at home, and told him the whole story—my relations with Vera and Princess Mary, and the conversation which I had overheard and from which I had learned the intention of these gentlemen to make a fool of me by causing me to fight a duel with blank cartridges. But, now, the affair had gone beyond the bounds of jest; they probably had not expected that it would turn out like this.

The doctor consented to be my second; I gave him a few directions with regard to the conditions of the duel. He was to insist upon the affair being managed with all possible secrecy, because, although I am prepared, at any moment, to face death, I am not in the least disposed to spoil for all time my future in this world.

After that I went home. In an hour's time the doctor returned from his expedition.

"There is indeed a conspiracy against you," he said. "I found the captain of dragoons at Grushnitski's, together with another gentleman whose surname I do not remember. I stopped a moment in the ante-room, in order to take off my goloshes. They were squabbling and making a terrible uproar. 'On no account will I agree,' Grushnitski was saying: 'he has insulted me publicly; it was quite a different thing before'...

"'What does it matter to you?' answered the captain. 'I will take it all upon myself. I have been second in five duels, and I should think I know how to arrange the affair. I have thought it all out. Just let me alone, please. It is not a bad thing to give people a bit of a fright. And why expose yourself to danger if it is possible to avoid it?'...

"At that moment I entered the room. They suddenly fell silent. Our negotiations were somewhat protracted. At length we decided the matter as follows: about five versts from here there is a hollow gorge; they will ride thither tomorrow at four o'clock in the morning, and we shall leave half an hour later. You will fire at six paces—Grushnitski himself demanded that condition. Whichever of you is killed—his death will be put down to the account of the Circassians. And now I must tell you what I suspect: they, that is to say the seconds, may have made some change in their former plan and may want to load only Grushnitski's pistol. That is something like murder, but in time of war, and especially in Asiatic warfare, such tricks are allowed. Grushnitski, however, seems to be a little more magnanimous than his companions. What do you think? Ought we not to let them see that we have guessed their plan?"

"Not on any account, doctor! Make your mind easy; I will not give in to them."

"But what are you going to do, then?"

"That is my secret."

"Mind you are not caught... six paces, you know!"

"Doctor, I shall expect you to-morrow at four o'clock. The horses will be ready... Goodbye."

I remained in the house until the evening, with my door locked. A manservant came to invite me to Princess Ligovski's—I bade him say that I was ill.

Two o'clock in the morning... I cannot sleep... Yet sleep is what I need, if I am to have a steady hand to-morrow. However, at six paces it is difficult to miss. Aha! Mr. Grushnitski, your wiles will not succeed!... We shall exchange roles: now it is I who shall have to seek the signs of latent terror upon your pallid countenance. Why have you yourself appointed these fatal six paces? Think you that I will tamely expose my forehead to your aim?...

No, we shall cast lots... And then—then—what if his luck should prevail? If my star at length should betray me?... And little wonder if it did: it has so long and faithfully served my caprices.

Well? If I must die, I must! The loss to the world will not be great; and I myself am already downright weary of everything. I am like a guest at a ball, who yawns but does not go home to bed, simply because his carriage has not come for him. But now the carriage is here... Good-bye!...

My whole past life I live again in memory, and, involuntarily, I ask myself: 'why have I lived—for what purpose was I born?'... A purpose there must have been, and, surely, mine was an exalted destiny, because I feel that within my soul are powers immeasurable... But I was not able to discover that destiny, I allowed myself to be carried away by the allurements of passions, inane and ignoble. From their crucible I issued hard and cold as iron, but gone forever was the glow of noble aspirations—the fairest flower of life. And, from that time forth, how often have I not played the part of an axe in the hands of fate! Like an implement of punishment, I have fallen upon the head of doomed victims, often without malice, always without pity... To none has my love brought happiness, because I have never sacrificed anything for the sake of those I have loved: for myself alone I have loved—for my own pleasure. I have only satisfied the strange craving of my heart, greedily draining their feelings, their tenderness, their joys, their sufferings—and I have never been able to sate myself. I am like one who, spent with hunger, falls asleep in exhaustion and sees before him sumptuous viands and sparkling wines; he devours with rapture the aerial gifts of the imagination, and his pains seem somewhat assuaged. Let him but awake: the vision vanishes—twofold hunger and despair remain!

And to-morrow, it may be, I shall die!... And there will not be left on earth one being who has understood me completely. Some will consider me worse, others, better, than I have been in reality... Some will say: 'he was a good fellow'; others: 'a villain.' And both epithets will be false. After all this, is life worth the trouble? And yet we live—out of curiosity! We expect something new... How absurd, and yet how vexatious!

# CHAPTER XIX

IT is now a month and a half since I have been in the N——Fortress.

Maksim Maksimych is out hunting... I am alone. I am sitting by the window. Grey clouds have covered the mountains to the foot; the sun appears through the mist as a yellow spot. It is cold; the wind is whistling and rocking the shutters... I am bored!... I will continue my diary which has been interrupted by so many strange events.

I read the last page over: how ridiculous it seems!... I thought to die; it was not to be. I have not yet drained the cup of suffering, and now I feel that I still have long to live.

How clearly and how sharply have all these bygone events been stamped upon my memory! Time has not effaced a single line, a single shade.

I remember that during the night preceding the duel I did not sleep a single moment. I was not able to write for long: a secret uneasiness took possession of me. For about an hour I paced the room, then I sat down and opened a novel by Walter Scott which was lying on my table. It was "The Scottish Puritans." [35] At first I read with an effort; then, carried away by the magical fiction, I became oblivious of everything else.

At last day broke. My nerves became composed. I looked in the glass: a dull pallor covered my face, which preserved the traces of harassing sleeplessness; but my eyes, although encircled by a brownish shadow, glittered proudly and inexorably. I was satisfied with myself.

I ordered the horses to be saddled, dressed myself, and ran down to the baths. Plunging into the cold, sparkling water of the Narzan Spring, I felt my bodily and mental powers returning. I left the baths as fresh and hearty as if I was off to a ball. After that, who shall say that the soul is not dependent upon the body!...

On my return, I found the doctor at my rooms. He was wearing grey riding-breeches, a jacket and a Circassian cap. I burst out laughing when I saw that little figure under the enormous shaggy cap. Werner has a by no means warlike countenance, and on that occasion it was even longer than usual.

---

[35] None of the Waverley novels, of course, bears this title. The novel referred to is doubtless "Old Mortality," on which Bellini's opera, "I Puritani di Scozia," is founded.

"Why so sad, doctor?" I said to him. "Have you not a hundred times, with the greatest indifference, escorted people to the other world? Imagine that I have a bilious fever: I may get well; also, I may die; both are in the usual course of things. Try to look on me as a patient, afflicted with an illness with which you are still unfamiliar—and then your curiosity will be aroused in the highest degree. You can now make a few important physiological observations upon me... Is not the expectation of a violent death itself a real illness?"

The doctor was struck by that idea, and he brightened up.

We mounted our horses. Werner clung on to his bridle with both hands, and we set off. In a trice we had galloped past the fortress, through the village, and had ridden into the gorge. Our winding road was half-overgrown with tall grass and was intersected every moment by a noisy brook, which we had to ford, to the great despair of the doctor, because each time his horse would stop in the water.

A morning more fresh and blue I cannot remember! The sun had scarce shown his face from behind the green summits, and the blending of the first warmth of his rays with the dying coolness of the night produced on all my feelings a sort of sweet languor. The joyous beam of the young day had not yet penetrated the gorge; it gilded only the tops of the cliffs which overhung us on both sides. The tufted shrubs, growing in the deep crevices of the cliffs, besprinkled us with a silver shower at the least breath of wind. I remember that on that occasion I loved Nature more than ever before. With what curiosity did I examine every dewdrop trembling upon the broad vine leaf and reflecting millions of rainbow-hued rays! How eagerly did my glance endeavor to penetrate the smoky distance! There the road grew narrower and narrower, the cliffs bluer and more dreadful, and at last they met, it seemed, in an impenetrable wall.

We rode in silence.

"Have you made your will?" Werner suddenly inquired.

"No."

"And if you are killed?"

"My heirs will be found of themselves."

"Is it possible that you have no friends, to whom you would like to send a last farewell?"...

I shook my head.

"Is there, really, not one woman in the world to whom you would like to leave some token in remembrance?"...

"Do you want me to reveal my soul to you, doctor?" I answered... "You see, I have outlived the years when people die with the name of the beloved on their lips and bequeathing to a friend a lock of pomaded—or un-pomaded—hair. When I think that death may be near, I think of myself alone; others do not even do as much. The friends who to-morrow will forget me or, worse, will utter goodness knows what falsehoods about me; the women who, while embracing another, will laugh at me in order not to arouse his jealousy of the deceased—let them go! Out of the storm of life I have borne away only a few ideas—and not one feeling. For a long time now I have been living, not with my heart, but with my head. I weigh, analyze my own passions and actions with severe curiosity, but without sympathy. There are two personalities within me: one lives—in the complete sense of the word—the other reflects and judges him; the first, it may be, in an hour's time, will take farewell of you and the world for ever, and the second—the second?... Look, doctor, do you see those three black figures on the cliff, to the right? They are our antagonists, I suppose?"...

We pushed on.

In the bushes at the foot of the cliff three horses were tethered; we tethered ours there too, and then we clambered up the narrow path to the ledge on which Grushnitski was awaiting us in company with the captain of dragoons and his other second, whom they called Ivan Ignatevich. His surname I never heard.

"We have been expecting you for quite a long time," said the captain of dragoons, with an ironical smile.

I drew out my watch and showed him the time.

He apologized, saying that his watch was fast.

There was an embarrassing silence for a few moments. At length the doctor interrupted it.

"It seems to me," he said, turning to Grushnitski, "that as you have both shown your readiness to fight, and thereby paid the debt due to the conditions of honor, you might be able to come to an explanation and finish the affair amicably."

"I am ready," I said.

The captain winked to Grushnitski, and the latter, thinking that I was losing courage, assumed a haughty air, although, until that moment, his cheeks had been covered with a dull pallor. For the first time since our arrival he lifted his eyes on me; but in his glance there was a certain disquietude which evinced an inward struggle.

"Declare your conditions," he said, "and anything I can do for you, be assured"...

"These are my conditions: you will this very day publicly recant your slander and beg my pardon"...

"My dear sir, I wonder how you dare make such a proposal to me?"

"What else could I propose?"...

"We will fight."

I shrugged my shoulders.

"Be it so; only, bethink you that one of us will infallibly be killed."

"I hope it will be you"...

"And I am so convinced of the contrary"...

He became confused, turned red, and then burst out into a forced laugh.

The captain took his arm and led him aside; they whispered together for a long time. I had arrived in a fairly pacific frame of mind, but all this was beginning to drive me furious.

The doctor came up to me.

"Listen," he said, with manifest uneasiness, "you have surely forgotten their conspiracy!... I do not know how to load a pistol, but in this case... You are a strange man! Tell them that you know their intention—and they will not dare... What sport! To shoot you like a bird"...

"Please do not be uneasy, doctor, and wait awhile... I shall arrange everything in such a way that there will be no advantage on their side. Let them whisper"...

"Gentlemen, this is becoming tedious," I said to them loudly: "if we are to fight, let us fight; you had time yesterday to talk as much as you wanted to."

"We are ready," answered the captain. "Take your places, gentlemen! Doctor, be good enough to measure six paces"...

"Take your places!" repeated Ivan Ignatevich, in a squeaky voice.

"Excuse me!" I said. "One further condition. As we are going to fight to the death, we are bound to do everything possible in order that the affair may remain a secret, and that our seconds may incur no responsibility. Do you agree?"...

"Quite."

"Well, then, this is my idea. Do you see that narrow ledge on the top of the perpendicular cliff on the right? It must be thirty fathoms, if not more, from there to the bottom; and, down below, there are sharp rocks. Each of us will stand right at the extremity of the ledge—in such manner even a slight wound will be mortal: that ought to be in accordance with your desire, as you yourselves have fixed upon six paces. Whichever of us is wounded will be certain to fall down and be dashed to pieces; the doctor will extract the bullet, and, then, it will be possible very easily to account for that sudden death by saying it was the result of a fall. Let us cast lots to decide who shall fire first. In conclusion, I declare that I will not fight on any other terms."

"Be it so!" said the captain after an expressive glance at Grushnitski, who nodded his head in token of assent. Every moment he was changing countenance. I had placed him in an embarrassing position. Had the duel been fought upon the usual conditions, he could have aimed at my leg, wounded me slightly, and in such wise gratified his vengeance without overburdening his conscience. But now he was obliged to fire in the air, or to make himself an assassin, or, finally, to abandon his base plan and to expose himself to equal danger with me. I should not have liked to be in his place at that moment. He took the captain aside and said something to him with great warmth. His lips were blue, and I saw them trembling; but the captain turned away from him with a contemptuous smile.

"You are a fool," he said to Grushnitski rather loudly. "You can't understand a thing!... Let us be off, then, gentlemen!"

The precipice was approached by a narrow path between bushes, and fragments of rock formed the precarious steps of that natural staircase. Clinging to the bushes we proceeded to clamber up. Grushnitski went in front, his seconds behind him, and then the doctor and I.

"I am surprised at you," said the doctor, pressing my hand vigorously. "Let me feel your pulse!... Oho! Feverish!... But nothing noticeable on your countenance... only your eyes are gleaming more brightly than usual."

Suddenly small stones rolled noisily right under our feet. What was it? Grushnitski had stumbled; the branch to which he was clinging had broken off, and he would have rolled down on his back if his seconds had not held him up.

"Take care!" I cried. "Do not fall prematurely: that is a bad sign. Remember Julius Caesar!"

# CHAPTER XX

AND now we had climbed to the summit of the projecting cliff. The ledge was covered with fine sand, as if on purpose for a duel. All around, like an innumerable herd, crowded the mountains, their summits lost to view in the golden mist of the morning; and towards the south rose the white mass of Elbruz, closing the chain of icy peaks, among which fibrous clouds, which had rushed in from the east, were already roaming. I walked to the extremity of the ledge and gazed down. My head nearly swam. At the foot of the precipice all seemed dark and cold as in a tomb; the moss-grown jags of the rocks, hurled down by storm and time, were awaiting their prey.

The ledge on which we were to fight formed an almost regular triangle. Six paces were measured from the projecting corner, and it was decided that whichever had first to meet the fire of his opponent should stand in the very corner with his back to the precipice; if he was not killed the adversaries would change places.

I determined to relinquish every advantage to Grushnitski; I wanted to test him. A spark of magnanimity might awake in his soul—and then all would have been settled for the best. But his vanity and weakness of character had perforce to triumph!... I wished to give myself the full right to refrain from sparing him if destiny were to favor me. Who would not have concluded such an agreement with his conscience?

"Cast the lot, doctor!" said the captain.

The doctor drew a silver coin from his pocket and held it up.

"Tail!" cried Grushnitski hurriedly, like a man suddenly aroused by a friendly nudge.

"Head," I said.

The coin spun in the air and fell, jingling. We all rushed towards it.

"You are lucky," I said to Grushnitski. "You are to fire first! But remember that if you do not kill me I shall not miss—I give you my word of honor."

He flushed up; he was ashamed to kill an unarmed man. I looked at him fixedly; for a moment it seemed to me that he would throw himself at my feet, imploring forgiveness; but how to confess so base a plot?... One expedient only was left to him—to fire in the air! I was convinced that he would fire in the air! One consideration alone might prevent him doing so—the thought that I would demand a second duel.

"Now is the time!" the doctor whispered to me, plucking me by the sleeve. "If you do not tell them now that we know their intentions, all is lost. Look, he is loading already... If you will not say anything, I will"...

"On no account, doctor!" I answered, holding him back by the arm. "You will spoil everything. You have given me your word not to interfere... What does it matter to you? Perhaps I wish to be killed"...

He looked at me in astonishment.

"Oh, that is another thing!... Only do not complain of me in the other world"...

Meanwhile the captain had loaded his pistols and given one to Grushnitski, after whispering something to him with a smile; the other he gave to me.

I placed myself in the corner of the ledge, planting my left foot firmly against the rock and bending slightly forward, so that, in case of a slight wound, I might not fall over backwards.

Grushnitski placed himself opposite me and, at a given signal, began to raise his pistol. His knees shook. He aimed right at my forehead... Unutterable fury began to seethe within my breast.

Suddenly he dropped the muzzle of the pistol and, pale as a sheet, turned to his second.

"I cannot," he said in a hollow voice.

"Coward!" answered the captain.

A shot rang out. The bullet grazed my knee. Involuntarily I took a few paces forward in order to get away from the edge as quickly as possible.

"Well, my dear Grushnitski, it is a pity that you have missed!" said the captain. "Now it is your turn, take your stand! Embrace me first: we shall not see each other again!"

They embraced; the captain could scarcely refrain from laughing.

"Do not be afraid," he added, glancing cunningly at Grushnitski; "everything in this world is nonsense... Nature is a fool, fate a turkeyhen, and life a copeck!" [36]

After that tragic phrase, uttered with becoming gravity, he went back to his place. Ivan Ignatevich, with tears, also embraced Grushnitski, and there the latter remained alone, facing me. Ever since then, I have been trying to explain to myself what sort of feeling it was that was boiling within my breast at that moment: it was the vexation of injured vanity, and contempt, and wrath engendered at the thought that the man now looking at me with such confidence, such quiet insolence, had, two minutes before, been about to kill me like a dog, without exposing himself to the least danger, because had I been wounded a little more severely in the leg I should inevitably have fallen over the cliff.

For a few moments I looked him fixedly in the face, trying to discern thereon even a slight trace of repentance. But it seemed to me that he was restraining a smile.

"I should advise you to say a prayer before you die," I said.

"Do not worry about my soul any more than your own. One thing I beg of you: be quick about firing."

"And you do not recant your slander? You do not beg my forgiveness?... Bethink you well: has your conscience nothing to say to you?"

"Mr. Pechorin!" exclaimed the captain of dragoons. "Allow me to point out that you are not here to preach... Let us lose no time, in case anyone should ride through the gorge and we should be seen."

"Very well. Doctor, come here!"

The doctor came up to me. Poor doctor! He was paler than Grushnitski had been ten minutes before.

The words which followed I purposely pronounced with a pause between each—loudly and distinctly, as the sentence of death is pronounced:

"Doctor, these gentlemen have forgotten, in their hurry, no doubt, to put a bullet in my pistol. I beg you to load it afresh—and properly!"

---

[36] Popular phrases, equivalent to: "Men are fools, fortune is blind, and life is not worth a straw."

"Impossible!" cried the captain, "impossible! I loaded both pistols. Perhaps the bullet has rolled out of yours... That is not my fault! And you have no right to load again... No right at all. It is altogether against the rules, I shall not allow it"...

"Very well!" I said to the captain. "If so, then you and I shall fight on the same terms"...

He came to a dead stop.

Grushnitski stood with his head sunk on his breast, embarrassed and gloomy.

"Let them be!" he said at length to the captain, who was going to pull my pistol out of the doctor's hands. "You know yourself that they are right."

In vain the captain made various signs to him. Grushnitski would not even look.

Meanwhile the doctor had loaded the pistol and handed it to me. On seeing that, the captain spat and stamped his foot.

"You are a fool, then, my friend," he said: "a common fool!... You trusted to me before, so you should obey me in everything now... But serve you right! Die like a fly!"...

He turned away, muttering as he went:

"But all the same it is absolutely against the rules."

"Grushnitski!" I said. "There is still time: recant your slander, and I will forgive you everything. You have not succeeded in making a fool of me; my self-esteem is satisfied. Remember—we were once friends"...

His face flamed, his eyes flashed.

"Fire!" he answered. "I despise myself and I hate you. If you do not kill me I will lie in wait for you some night and cut your throat. There is not room on the earth for both of us"...

I fired.

When the smoke had cleared away, Grushnitski was not to be seen on the ledge. Only a slender column of dust was still eddying at the edge of the precipice.

There was a simultaneous cry from the rest.

"Finita la commedia!" I said to the doctor.

He made no answer, and turned away with horror.

I shrugged my shoulders and bowed to Grushnitski's seconds.

# CHAPTER XXI

AS I descended by the path, I observed Grushnitski's bloodstained corpse between the clefts of the rocks. Involuntarily, I closed my eyes.

Untying my horse, I set off home at a walking pace. A stone lay upon my heart. To my eyes the sun seemed dim, its beams were powerless to warm me.

I did not ride up to the village, but turned to the right, along the gorge. The sight of a man would have been painful to me: I wanted to be alone. Throwing down the bridle and letting my head fall on my breast, I rode for a long time, and at length found myself in a spot with which I was wholly unfamiliar. I turned my horse back and began to search for the road. The sun had already set by the time I had ridden up to Kislovodsk—myself and my horse both utterly spent!

My servant told me that Werner had called, and he handed me two notes: one from Werner, the other... from Vera.

I opened the first; its contents were as follows:

"Everything has been arranged as well as could be; the mutilated body has been brought in; and the bullet extracted from the breast. Everybody is convinced that the cause of death was an unfortunate accident; only the Commandant, who was doubtless aware of your quarrel, shook his head, but he said nothing. There are no proofs at all against you, and you may sleep in peace... if you can.... Farewell!"...

For a long time I could not make up my mind to open the second note... What could it be that she was writing to me?... My soul was agitated by a painful foreboding.

Here it is, that letter, each word of which is indelibly engraved upon my memory:

"I am writing to you in the full assurance that we shall never see each other again. A few years ago on parting with you I thought the same. However, it has been Heaven's will to try me a second time: I have not been able to endure the trial, my frail heart has again submitted to the well-known voice... You will not despise me for that—will you? This letter will be at once a farewell and a confession: I am obliged to tell you everything that has been treasured up in my heart since it began to love you. I will not accuse you—you have acted towards me as any other man would have acted; you have loved me as a chattel, as a source of joys, disquietudes and griefs, interchanging one with the other, without which life would be dull and monotonous. I have understood all that from the first... But you were unhappy, and I have sacrificed myself, hoping that, some time, you would appreciate my sacrifice, that some time you would understand my deep tenderness, unfettered by any conditions. A long time has elapsed since then: I have fathomed all the secrets of your soul... and I have convinced myself that my hope was vain. It has been a bitter blow to me! But my love has been grafted with my soul; it has grown dark, but has not been extinguished.

"We are parting forever; yet you may be sure that I shall never love another. Upon you my soul has exhausted all its treasures, its tears, its hopes. She who has once loved you cannot look without a certain disdain upon other men, not because you have been better than they, oh, no! but in your nature there is something peculiar—belonging to you alone, something proud and mysterious; in your voice, whatever the words spoken, there is an invincible power. No one can so constantly wish to be loved, in no one is wickedness ever so attractive, no one's glance promises so much bliss, no one can better make use of his advantages, and no one can be so truly unhappy as you, because no one endeavors so earnestly to convince himself of the contrary.

"Now I must explain the cause of my hurried departure; it will seem of little importance to you, because it concerns me alone.

"This morning my husband came in and told me about your quarrel with Grushnitski. Evidently I changed countenance greatly, because he looked me in the face long and intently. I almost fainted at the thought that you had to fight a duel to-day, and that I was the cause of it; it seemed to me that I should go mad... But now, when I am able to reason, I am sure that you remain alive: it is impossible that you should die, and I not with you—impossible! My husband walked about the room for a long time. I do not know what he said to me, I do not remember what I answered... Most likely I told him that I loved you... I only remember that, at the end of our conversation, he insulted me with a dreadful word and left the room. I heard him ordering the carriage... I have been sitting at the window three hours now, awaiting your return... But you are alive, you cannot have died!... The carriage is almost ready... Good-bye, good-bye!... I have perished—but what matter? If I could be sure that you will always remember me—I no longer say love—no, only remember... Good-bye, they are coming!... I must hide this letter.

"You do not love Mary, do you? You will not marry her? Listen, you must offer me that sacrifice. I have lost everything in the world for you"...

Like a madman I sprang on the steps, jumped on my Circassian horse which was being led about the courtyard, and set off at full gallop along the road to Pyatigorsk. Unsparingly I urged on the jaded horse, which, snorting and all in a foam, carried me swiftly along the rocky road.

The sun had already disappeared behind a black cloud, which had been resting on the ridge of the western mountains; the gorge grew dark and damp. The Podkumok, forcing its way over the rocks, roared with a hollow and monotonous sound. I galloped on, choking with impatience. The idea of not finding Vera in Pyatigorsk struck my heart like a hammer. For one minute, again to see her for one minute, to say farewell, to press her hand... I prayed, cursed, wept, laughed... No, nothing could express my anxiety, my despair!... Now that it seemed possible that I might be about to lose her forever, Vera became dearer to me than aught in the world—dearer than life, honor, happiness! God knows what strange, what mad plans swarmed in my head... Meanwhile I still galloped, urging on my horse without pity. And, now, I began to notice that he was breathing more heavily; he had already stumbled once or twice on level ground... I was five versts from Essentuki—a Cossack village where I could change horses.

All would have been saved had my horse been able to hold out for another ten minutes. But suddenly, in lifting himself out of a little gulley where the road emerges from the mountains at a sharp turn, he fell to the ground. I jumped down promptly, I tried to lift him up, I tugged at his bridle—in vain. A scarcely audible moan burst through his clenched teeth; in a few moments he expired. I was left on the steppe, alone; I had lost my last hope. I endeavored to walk—my legs sank under me; exhausted by the anxieties of the day and by sleeplessness, I fell upon the wet grass and burst out crying like a child.

For a long time I lay motionless and wept bitterly, without attempting to restrain my tears and sobs. I thought my breast would burst. All my firmness, all my coolness, disappeared like smoke; my soul grew powerless, my reason silent, and, if anyone had seen me at that moment, he would have turned aside with contempt.

When the night-dew and the mountain breeze had cooled my burning brow, and my thoughts had resumed their usual course, I realized that to pursue my perished happiness would be unavailing and unreasonable. What more did I want?—To see her?—Why? Was not all over between us?

A single, bitter, farewell kiss would not have enriched my recollections, and, after it, parting would only have been more difficult for us.

Still, I am pleased that I can weep. Perhaps, however, the cause of that was my shattered nerves, a night passed without sleep, two minutes opposite the muzzle of a pistol, and an empty stomach.

It is all for the best. That new suffering created within me a fortunate diversion—to speak in military style. To weep is healthy, and then, no doubt, if I had not ridden as I did and had not been obliged to walk fifteen versts on my way back, sleep would not have closed my eyes on that night either.

I returned to Kislovodsk at five o'clock in the morning, threw myself on my bed, and slept the sleep of Napoleon after Waterloo.

By the time I awoke it was dark outside. I sat by the open window, with my jacket unbuttoned—and the mountain breeze cooled my breast, still troubled by the heavy sleep of weariness. In the distance beyond the river, through the tops of the thick lime trees which overshadowed it, lights were glancing in the fortress and the village. Close at hand all was calm. It was dark in Princess Ligovski's house.

The doctor entered; his brows were knit; contrary to custom, he did not offer me his hand.

"Where have you come from, doctor?"

"From Princess Ligovski's; her daughter is ill—nervous exhaustion... That is not the point, though. This is what I have come to tell you: the authorities are suspicious, and, although it is impossible to prove anything positively, I should, all the same, advise you to be cautious. Princess Ligovski told me to-day that she knew that you fought a duel on her daughter's account. That little old man—what's his name?—has told her everything. He was a witness of your quarrel with Grushnitski in the restaurant. I have come to warn you. Good-bye. Maybe we shall not meet again: you will be banished somewhere."

He stopped on the threshold; he would gladly have pressed my hand... and, had I shown the slightest desire to embrace him, he would have thrown himself upon my neck; but I remained cold as a rock—and he left the room.

That is just like men! They are all the same: they know beforehand all the bad points of an act, they help, they advise, they even encourage it, seeing the impossibility of any other expedient—and then they wash their hands of the whole affair and turn away with indignation from him who has had the courage to take the whole burden of responsibility upon himself. They are all like that, even the best-natured, the wisest...

# CHAPTER XXII

NEXT morning, having received orders from the supreme authority to betake myself to the N——Fortress, I called upon Princess Ligovski to say good-bye.

She was surprised when, in answer to her question, whether I had not anything of special importance to tell her, I said I had come to wish her good-bye, and so on.

"But I must have a very serious talk with you."

I sat down in silence.

It was clear that she did not know how to begin; her face grew livid, she tapped the table with her plump fingers; at length, in a broken voice, she said:

"Listen, Monsieur Pechorin, I think that you are a gentleman."

I bowed.

"Nay, I am sure of it," she continued, "although your behaviour is somewhat equivocal, but you may have reasons which I do not know; and you must now confide them to me. You have protected my daughter from slander, you have fought a duel on her behalf—consequently you have risked your life... Do not answer. I know that you will not acknowledge it because Grushnitski has been killed"—she crossed herself. "God forgive him—and you too, I hope... That does not concern me... I dare not condemn you because my daughter, although innocently, has been the cause. She has told me everything... everything, I think. You have declared your love for her... She has admitted hers to you."—Here Princess Ligovski sighed heavily.—"But she is ill, and I am certain that it is no simple illness! Secret grief is killing her; she will not confess, but I am convinced that you are the cause of it... Listen: you think, perhaps, that I am looking for rank or immense wealth—be undeceived, my daughter's happiness is my sole desire. Your present position is unenviable, but it may be bettered: you have means; my daughter loves you; she has been brought up in such a way

147

that she will make her husband a happy man. I am wealthy, she is my only child... Tell me, what is keeping you back?... You see, I ought not to be saying all this to you, but I rely upon your heart, upon your honor—remember she is my only daughter... my only one"...

She burst into tears.

"Princess," I said, "it is impossible for me to answer you; allow me to speak to your daughter, alone"...

"Never!" she exclaimed, rising from her chair in violent agitation.

"As you wish," I answered, preparing to go away.

She fell into thought, made a sign to me with her hand that I should wait a little, and left the room.

Five minutes passed. My heart was beating violently, but my thoughts were tranquil, my head cool. However assiduously I sought in my breast for even a spark of love for the charming Mary, my efforts were of no avail!

Then the door opened, and she entered. Heavens! How she had changed since I had last seen her—and that but a short time ago!

When she reached the middle of the room, she staggered. I jumped up, gave her my arm, and led her to a chair.

I stood facing her. We remained silent for a long time; her large eyes, full of unutterable grief, seemed to be searching in mine for something resembling hope; her wan lips vainly endeavored to smile; her tender hands, which were folded upon her knees, were so thin and transparent that I pitied her.

"Princess," I said, "you know that I have been making fun of you?... You must despise me."

A sickly flush suffused her cheeks.

"Consequently," I continued, "you cannot love me"...

She turned her head away, leaned her elbows on the table, covered her eyes with her hand, and it seemed to me that she was on the point of tears.

"Oh, God!" she said, almost inaudibly.

The situation was growing intolerable. Another minute—and I should have fallen at her feet.

148

"So you see, yourself," I said in as firm a voice as I could command, and with a forced smile, "you see, yourself, that I cannot marry you. Even if you wished it now, you would soon repent. My conversation with your mother has compelled me to explain myself to you so frankly and so brutally. I hope that she is under a delusion: it will be easy for you to undeceive her. You see, I am playing a most pitiful and ugly role in your eyes, and I even admit it—that is the utmost I can do for your sake. However bad an opinion you may entertain of me, I submit to it... You see that I am base in your sight, am I not?... Is it not true that, even if you have loved me, you would despise me from this moment?"...

She turned round to me. She was pale as marble, but her eyes were sparkling wondrously.

"I hate you"... she said.

I thanked her, bowed respectfully, and left the room.

An hour afterwards a postal express was bearing me rapidly from Kislovodsk. A few versts from Essentuki I recognized near the roadway the body of my spirited horse. The saddle had been taken off, no doubt by a passing Cossack, and, in its place, two ravens were sitting on the horse's back. I sighed and turned away...

And now, here in this wearisome fortress, I often ask myself, as my thoughts wander back to the past: why did I not wish to tread that way, thrown open by destiny, where soft joys and ease of soul were awaiting me?... No, I could never have become habituated to such a fate! I am like a sailor born and bred on the deck of a pirate brig: his soul has grown accustomed to storms and battles; but, once let him be case upon the shore, and he chafes, he pines away, however invitingly the shady groves allure, however brightly shines the peaceful sun. The livelong day he paces the sandy shore, hearkens to the monotonous murmur of the onrushing waves, and gazes into the misty distance: lo! yonder, upon the pale line dividing the blue deep from the grey clouds, is there not glancing the longed-for sail, at first like the wing of a seagull, but little by little severing itself from the foam of the billows and, with even course, drawing nigh to the desert harbor?

# APPENDIX

## PREFACE TO THE SECOND EDITION
## (By the Author)

THE preface to a book serves the double purpose of prologue and epilogue. It affords the author an opportunity of explaining the object of the work, or of vindicating himself and replying to his critics. As a rule, however, the reader is concerned neither with the moral purpose of the book nor with the attacks of the Reviewers, and so the preface remains unread. Nevertheless, this is a pity, especially with us Russians! The public of this country is so youthful, not to say simple-minded, that it cannot understand the meaning of a fable unless the moral is set forth at the end. Unable to see a joke, insensible to irony, it has, in a word, been badly brought up. It has not yet learned that in a decent book, as in decent society, open invective can have no place; that our present-day civilization has invented a keener weapon, none the less deadly for being almost invisible, which, under the cloak of flattery, strikes with sure and irresistible effect. The Russian public is like a simple-minded person from the country who, chancing to overhear a conversation between two diplomatists belonging to hostile courts, comes away with the conviction that each of them has been deceiving his Government in the interest of a most affectionate private friendship.

The unfortunate effects of an over-literal acceptation of words by certain readers and even Reviewers have recently been manifested in regard to the present book. Many of its readers have been dreadfully, and in all seriousness, shocked to find such an immoral man as Pechorin set before them as an example. Others have observed, with much acumen, that the author has painted his own portrait and those of his acquaintances!... What a stale and wretched jest! But Russia, it appears, has been constituted in such a way that absurdities of this kind will never be eradicated. It is doubtful whether, in this country, the most ethereal of fairy-tales would escape the reproach of attempting offensive personalities.

Pechorin, gentlemen, is in fact a portrait, but not of one man only: he is a composite portrait, made up of all the vices which flourish, fullgrown, amongst the present generation. You will tell me, as you have told me before, that no man can be so bad as this; and my reply will be: "If you believe that such persons as the villains of tragedy and romance could exist in real life, why can you not believe in the reality of Pechorin? If you

150

admire fictions much more terrible and monstrous, why is it that this character, even if regarded merely as a creature of the imagination, cannot obtain quarter at your hands? Is it not because there is more truth in it than may be altogether palatable to you?"

You will say that the cause of morality gains nothing by this book. I beg your pardon. People have been surfeited with sweetmeats and their digestion has been ruined: bitter medicines, sharp truths, are therefore necessary. This must not, however, be taken to mean that the author has ever proudly dreamed of becoming a reformer of human vices. Heaven keep him from such impertinence! He has simply found it entertaining to depict a man, such as he considers to be typical of the present day and such as he has often met in real life—too often, indeed, unfortunately both for the author himself and for you. Suffice it that the disease has been pointed out: how it is to be cured—God alone knows!

Made in United States
North Haven, CT
19 April 2022